Out of Thin Air

Also by Alex Jack

Dragon Brood: An Epic Play about Vietnam and America
The Adamantine Sherlock Holmes
The New Age Dictionary
Let Food Be Thy Medicine
Inspector Ginkgo, the Macrobiotic Sherlock Holmes

with Gale Jack
Promenade Home
Amber Waves of Grain

with Michio Kushi
The Cancer-Prevention Diet
Diet for a Strong Heart
One Peaceful World
The Book of Macrobiotics
The Gospel of Peace

with Aveline Kushi
Complete Guide to Macrobiotic Cooking
Aveline: The Life and Dream of the Woman
Behind Macrobiotics Today

with Michio and Aveline Kushi
Macrobiotic Diet
Food Governs Your Destiny

with Norman Ralston, D.V.M.
The Natural Dog and Cat Book

Out of Thin Air

By Alex Jack

One Peaceful World Press
Becket, Massachusetts

Out of Thin Air
© 1993 by Alex Jack

All rights reserved, including dramatic and performing rights. Printed in the United States of America. No part of this book may be used or reproduced in any manner whatsoever without written permission except in the case of brief quotations embodied in critical articles or reviews or skits or adaptations performed by children. For information, contact the publisher.

Published by One Peaceful World, Becket, Massachusetts, U.S.A.

For further information on mail-order sales, wholesale or retail discounts, distribution, translations, foreign rights, and dramatic and performing rights, please contact the publisher:

One Peaceful World Press
P.O. Box 10
308 Leland Road
Becket, MA 01223
U.S.A.

Telephone (413) 623-2322
Fax (413) 623-8827

First Edition: January 1993
10 9 8 7 6 5 4 3 2 1

ISBN 0-9628528-7-2
Printed in U.S.A.

To Masha with love

"Owl—in days to come humans will listen to your voice to know what will be their future."
—Native American legend

Author's Note

The world's average temperature today is only about 3 degrees warmer than it was during the last ice age. In the next thirty years, the earth's temperature is expected to rise another 3 degrees. This is the result of the rapid spread of modern civilization, or what has come to be known as the Greenhouse Effect. This dramatic increase—taking place over a few decades, not thousands or millions of years as in the past—could result in profound changes in life on earth during our lifetime and that of our children. *Out of Thin Air* presents a satirical look at what life might be like then—one scenario among many that hopefully will be averted. Humanity can pass safely through this unprecedented crisis if we start to take responsibility for our personal, social, and environmental health and learn to live as a planetary family. Common sense and merry, good humor will help see us through. To this end, this book is devoted.

The author is grateful to Michio and Aveline Kushi for their continual guidance and inspiration, to his associates at the Kushi Institute and One Peaceful World Press, especially Edward and Wendy Esko, for their encouragement, and to his wife, Gale, and family for their love and support.

> Alex Jack
> One Peaceful World Village
> Becket, Massachusetts
> Autumn 1992

Cast

Noah Wilson, a New York advertising executive
   Kathy, his wife
   Jason, their older son
   Mark, their younger son
   Maggie, their older daughter
   Emily, their younger daughter
Krishna Deva, a cab driver
Daryl, manager of a McDonald's
Marty, a policeman
Shiva Deva, a judge
   Parvati, his wife
   Maya, his courtroom assistant
   Nandi, his bull
Prosecuter
Witnesses
   Dr. Albert Salisbury, New York physician
   Sara Dunlap, Nebraska schoolgirl
   Ibraham Salim, Pakistani filmmaker
   Li Wei, Chinese drug and alcohol rehabilitiation official
   Carlos "Big Tofu" Martinique, ex-Latin American drug king
   Rebecca Mir, Israeli soldier
   Ellen Schwartz, Utah aeromobile executive
   Mwalimu Tombo, African farmer
   Yuri Volshoya, Russian nuclear scientist
   Aii Xingu, Rain forest healer
   Glenn Hammock, Canadian climatologist
   Tex Waylor, singing cowboy and film star
Jury
Great Spotted Owl
Brahma Deva, a doctor

1

Setting: the home of Noah Wilson and his family in southern Connecticut. The time is the early 1990s. Noah, an advertising executive, is getting ready to leave for the airport and an important business meeting in Seattle. It is the middle of the summer and very hot.

Noah: Honey, can you turn up the air conditioning. It's hotter than hell.

Kathy: It's as high as it will go, Noah.

Noah: What's that smell?

Kathy: It's the air blowing in from the Sound. There was another red algae alert, and they closed the beach down. I'm sorry, sweetie, but I had to open the windows when the power failed.

Noah: Stepping out of the shower with a towel and deodorant spray and looking out the window to the neighbor's lawn. The Steadmans have their sprinkler on again. No wonder we have so many brown outs.

Kathy: Some people are so inconsiderate.

Noah: I was really hoping to take a spin in the water. I hope the marina is cleaned up by the weekend.

Kathy: Don't forget to take the extra shirt I laid out for you, Sweetie.

Noah: I'll probably need a change by the time I get to the airport. What's for dinner, honey?

Kathy: I'm sorry, Noah, but I'm running behind in the kitchen again. The power was down for a couple hours this afternoon, and I had three big loads of laundry. Then the microwave crashed and needs a new element. How about a nice piece of cheesecake?

Noah: Looking at his watch. No thanks, Honey. I don't have time to eat anyway. The cab'll be here in a moment. Besides, it's safer to swim with the sharks on an empty stomach.

Kathy: Maybe you can grab something at the airport.

The doorbell rings and Noah runs to the front door with his briefcase. However, his oldest son, Jason, beats him to the door.

Jason: Chill out, Dad. It's just the pizza man.

Noah: *Looks at his watch.* His next delivery isn't on Long Island by any chance?

Jason: Dad, can I have ten bucks?

Noah: What did you order—pizza with truffles and paté de foie gras?

Jason: The deluxe with triple pepperoni. Remember, Coach told me I'd have to put on 30 pounds this summer if I wanted a shot at making all-state tackle this year.

Noah: *Handing him the money.* Did Coach also tell you how much it would cost your poor father to become All-Beef?

Jason: Hey, lighten up, Pop. Don't be so pennywise and pound foolish. If I win an athletic scholarship to UConn, it'll save you 25 grand a year.

Noah: *Takes out another bill and hands it to Jason.* On second thought, have some more pepperoni.

Maggie, Harry's older daughter, comes in munching an ice cream cone.

Maggie: Daddy, can I get a mo-ped?

Noah: What's wrong with your bicycle, dear?

Maggie: Too slow. I really need something faster. Besides, it's more fuel-efficient than a car.

Noah: I know, don't tell me. I'll be saving myself ten grand if I get you a moped instead of a Mazda. *Aside to himself.* What ever happened to ponies? Don't little girls go through a horsie stage any more? *Pats her on the shoulder.* You know Daddy's working on his boat in the garage this summer, and there isn't any room for another vehicle right now. Now finish your ice cream and get back to your homework. *She goes off pouting.*

Kathy: I wish you didn't have to go to Seattle, Noah.

Noah: You know I hate missing Mark's birthday tomorrow.

Kathy: It's not the party, Noah. It's just not like you to take a client like that.

Noah: *Defensively.* Like what? Olympia Paper is one of the oldest and most reputable companies in the country. And since that anti-cancer drug was synthesized from the yew tree, the AMA and American Cancer Society are now involved.

Kathy: Does that justify cutting down whole forests and endangering numerous species?

Noah: We've been through this before, Kathy. It's more complicated than it looks.

Kathy: What happened to the man I married, the one I met stenciling wallposters during the Harvard Strike? The Noah Wilson who was a rising star on Madison Avenue and walked away from the R. J. Reynolds account and set up his own ad agency? The Noah Wilson who over the years has done *pro bono* work for the nuclear freeze and the South African boycott?

Noah: Sometimes you have to make hard choices, Kathy. Life is a trade off. I like trees as much as anyone, but I happen to believe people are more important than animals and plants.

Kathy: It doesn't have to be one or the other.

Noah: You make me feel like I'm masterminding the Willie Horton campaign or going to bat for Dow Chemical.

Kathy: I don't meant to nag you, but you have this stubborn streak, Noah, and won't back down when it's clearly the right thing to do.

She opens the door and the stench is overpowering.

Kathy: When we moved to the suburbs to bring up our family in a clean, natural environment, I never imagined this.

Noah: You make me feel like a Yuppie twit, Kathy. The work I'm doing now is just as visionary as ever.

Kathy: I hope so, dear. For all our sakes.

Noah: Believe me, in thirty years the earth will be completely changed—for the better. Our children will be living in a paradise. What I wouldn't give to see it.

Emily, Noah's youngest daughter, comes in. She is clutching a toy stuffed owl.

Noah: Hi, Sunshine. *He takes her owl and puts it out of sight as it reminds him of the logging controversy.*

Emily: Daddy, what's the Greenhouse Effect?

Noah: What is this, *Meet the Press*?

Emily: Please, Daddy, I want to know for my science camp.

Noah: It's when too much pollution builds up in the atmosphere and the environment becomes overheated.

Emily: Like in our house? *She points to the humidity condensing on the windows.*

Noah: *Laughs.* Yeh, Sunshine, but we're talking about planetary scale. In extreme cases, the icecaps could melt, coastal areas flood, and the axis might shift.

Kathy: *Wiping her brow of perspiration.* Cab's here, Noah. Have a safe journey.

Noah: Bye, honey. Bye, kids. *He notices the younger son is missing.* By the way, where's Mark?

Kathy: The junior investment club meets tonight and he stopped off at McDonald's with his friends. I asked him to pick up the element for the microwave at the hardware's on the way back.

Noah: *Aside.* Why can't he play Little League like other 12-year-olds? *To Kathy.* Well, tell him I'm sorry to miss his party, but I'll be back on Saturday and we'll have a big barbeque on the Fourth. Oh, yeh, and tell him to check out Genetech and Agricom. The sky's the limit.

Noah's youngest daughter enters the room.

Emily: Papa, take this, in case it gets too warm. *She hands him a little folding fan.*

Noah: *She holds up her stuffed animal to be kissed.* Thanks, Sunshine. Ciao, owl.

The cab out front honks and Noah goes out the front door.

2

In the cab on the way to Kennedy Airport. The driver, Krishna Deva, is an Indian. He has long hair, a necklace, long cotton tunic, and his legs are drawn up in the driver's seat in a full lotus.

Noah: Take me to Kennedy Airport and step on it. I'm in a hurry.

Krishna: Everybody's in a hurry in the Kali Yuga.

Noah: *Looking up at the driver for the first time.* Say, are you from India?

Krishna: I'm called Krishna Deva, and I originally came from Bangalore. Now I live in the Bronx.

Noah: Just the other day in the *Times*, there was a story about how half the cabbies in New York are now from India or Pakistan. What were you in India—a surgeon or a rocket scientist?

Krishna: A lawyer.

Noah: Well, driving a cab is honest work, and over here there are no holy cows on the streets to hit. *Laughs.* They're all behind the bench.

Krishna: Judge not lest ye be judged.

Noah: Spare me the philosophizing, Krishna, old man. But I've got an important meeting in Seattle and have to crunch some numbers. *Takes out his laptop computer and hands Krishna a five dollar bill.* Here's a little something for your trouble. Enjoy a pizza on me.

Krishna: I don't eat pizza.

Noah: *Startled.* What? Everybody in this country eats pizza? How do you expect to litigate before the Supreme Court without eating pizza?

Krishna: I'm a strict vegetarian.

Noah: I suppose that's why you're so lean. Well, use it to buy a bowl of rice or whatever it is you eat. Just get me to Northwest by quarter to seven, alright?

Krishna: *Chanting from the Upanishads.*
From food are born all creatures.
They live upon food.
They are dissolved in food.

Food is the chief of all things,
The universal medicine.
Who knows this, knows.

Noah: *Annoyed at how hot it's getting.* Would you mind turning up the air conditioner, Mr. K.? I can hardly think in this heat.

Krishna: *Fiddles with the controls and chants again from the Bhagavad Gita.*
The higher self of a tranquil person
whose mind is disciplined
is perfectly balanced in cold or heat,
joy or suffering,
gridlock or an open highway.

Noah: What's that, the revisionist version of the *Bhagavad Gita*?

Krishna: You know the *Gita*?

Noah: I read it in college a long time ago. I used to burn incense, wear love beads, and do a little yoga, believe it or not?

Krishna: You meditate?

Noah: Only about girls. I met Kathy, my future wife, at an ashram in Cambridge.

Krishna: Ever have a guru?

Noah: No, they were all hucksters.

Krishna: You turned within for truth?

Noah: *Laughs.* You could say I became my own huckster.

Krishna: That's cool.

Noah: Sounds like you went through a beat phase yourself?

Krishna: *Putting on some sunglasses from the dashboard and flicking on a jazz station on the radio.* You could say I am an old dharma bum at heart.

Noah: *Perplexed at the lack of perspiration on Krishna's shirt compared to his own and at Krishna's equanimity.* Say, you really are cool. Do you do TM or levitate?

Krishna: *Chants from the Gita.*
When he gives up striving with his mind,
is content with the self alone,
then he is said to be a man
whose insight and understanding are sure.

Noah: *Traffic has come to a halt. Noah looks frantically around in all directions.* It is getting hotter and hotter in the car. God, my computer's overheating. If I lose these numbers, my whole presentation could fall through. I knew I should have backed up the hard disk.

Krishna: *Turns around and takes the fan out of Noah's pocket.* Everything you need is very simple and close at hand.

Noah stares at it blankly until Krishna opens it up and makes fanning motions.

Noah: *Frantically fanning the computer.* The spreadsheet is coming back up. Krishna, you've saved my bacon!

Krishna: Maybe it would be better if you didn't make the meeting?

Noah: *Startled.* What makes you say that?

Krishna: The vibes. When things start acting peculiarly, karma is not far away.

Noah: *Defensively.* What are you, an animal rights activist? Sure, some tree huggers oppose the deal. But it's not like Love Canal. The trees will be replanted and the owls will be relocated. Meanwhile the doctors are happy. They will have their new anti-cancer drug, the loggers will go back to work and be able to support their families, the mills will stay open, and the Japanese who are financing the venture will be rolling in disposable chopsticks all the way to the Nikkei. Everyone prospers.

Krishna: *Chants from the Gita.*
An ignorant person is lost, rudderless,
and filled with self-doubt;
a soul that harbors doubt knows no joy,
neither in this world nor the world to come.
You don't sound convinced.

Noah: *Sinks down dejectedly in the back of the cab.* I'm not. It's awful. I'm caught in the middle and don't know which way to go. On one side are my wife and family and a lot of my friends who are environmentalists, and on the other is medical science and the economy.

Krishna: I'd like to help you, — ?

Noah: Noah, Noah Wilson.

Krishna: Your parents were missionaries, isn't it?

Noah: *Laughs.* Hardly. They turned to the dictionary to select a name for me, and I was hollaring so much they didn't get beyond the cover. They named me after Noah Webster.

Krishna: Rise up, Noah, and fight for what you truly believe in. Don't be influenced by what others think.

Noah: Last night I dreamed I was in a tree with my family. We were owls, and all around there was the sound of chainsaws.

Krishna: Karma leads all creatures to their destiny. Those who are blind to natural order and grasping are already destroyed. Those who believe in themselves and act righteously without attachment to their actions will win immortal glory.

Noah: Why are we moving so slowly?

Krishna: One of the levels of the Bridge ahead is out. At this rate, we'll be lucky to get to Shea Stadium by tomorrow morning.

Noah: *A surge of courage and determination comes over Noah.* God, if I don't make the reception tonight, my sushi's cooked. They may go with that other agency. There's got to be another way.

Can you suggest something?

The cab inches toward the Triborough Bridge. A big sign indicates that the upper level is closed for repairs, and the traffic going single file in the lower level has come to a complete halt. Ignoring the sign and roadblocks, Krishna heads for the closed off level.

Krishna: *Chants from the Gita.*
   Whoever offers a leaf, a flower petal,
   a grain of rice, or a drop of water,
   with devotion is dear to me.
   Starts to chant Aum. I think I know a short cut.

Still fanning his computer, Noah loosens his collar and sits back as the cab speeds onto the cloud-swept bridge.

3

Emerging from the bridge, Noah notices how clear the sky is and how balmy the temperature.

Noah: We really left the traffic behind, Krishna, didn't we? It almost feels like a new world. Calm, peaceful.

Krishna: Noah, this old chariot is faster than it looks.

Noah: *Looking at his watch.* I'll be damned, we're almost an hour early for the plane.

Krishna: Yama waits for no man.

Noah: You don't suppose there's a place to stop and get a bite? I'm starved.

Krishna: There's a McDonald's just up the road.

They pull up to a futuristic looking restaurant and stop.

Noah: Funny, I don't remember passing this place before. Must be one of those prefab places they put up overnight.

Krishna: It's been here at least thirty years.

Noah: No kidding? And what happened to the golden arches? They're green. Acid rain must have worn away the paint. I'll just go in and grab a hamburger. Care for anything?

Krishna: *Chants from the Gita.*
Attached to pleasures and might,
their mind lost in words,
they do not find in meditation
this knowledge of inner resolve.

Noah: Sorry, Counselor, I forgot, you eat veggie. How about some lettuce or onions? You look a little blue around the edges.

Krishna: *Chants from the Gita.*
When suffering does not disturb his thoughts,
when his appetite for delights has vanished,
when attachment, fear, and anger are spent,
he is called a sage whose mind is steady.

Noah: Be back in five.

Krishna: *Chants from the Gita.*
Sensuous pleasures fade
when the embodied self abstains from food;
the desire lingers, but it too fades
in the vision of universal order.

Noah enters the restaurant. There is a middle-aged man behind the counter cutting vegetables. His name, Daryl, is stitched on his work shirt. A few patrons are eating quietly, but the place is sparcely filled.

Daryl: Can I help you? Today's specials . . .

Noah: *Cutting him off.* I'm in a hurry, Jack. Let me have a burger with all the trimmings and double mustard and catsup. And a Coke to go.

Daryl: Sure thing. Would you like that a tofu burger, quinoa burger, sorghum burger, veggie burger, or a Big Macro—that's a burger made with brown rice and wild rice that's been fried with carrots and scallions? *Points to menu.* We've got twelve kinds in all.

Noah: *Aside.* What is this? McDonald's is test-marketing vegetarian food. I've heard they will introduce some new items and see if they fly. *Looks around.* Kind of people who eat a lot of bottled water and sprouts. Smart marketing move. *To Daryl.* No, give me just a regular hamburger. No frills.

Daryl: You sure you don't want a tempeh burger. It's very filling. It's my favorite.

Noah: No, just a good old All-American beef burger will do. *Aside.* Like father, like son.

Daryl: Well, it's a free planet, Mister. *Takes a beef patty out of a small refrigerated wall safe and puts it in the oven.* One hamburger coming up.

Noah: *Noticing the novel design and construction of the oven.* That's some spiffy microwave you've got. I've never seen one like that before.

Daryl: It's a solar oven.

Noah: No kidding. The electric rates must be higher here on the Island than they are in Connecticut.

Daryl: Actually, most of our electricity is generated from wind farms.

Noah: I had no idea how sophisticated solar and wind power had become since the '60s. You mean it's cost effective?

Daryl: You bet, it's just a fraction of what was once spent on oil, gas, and nuclear.

Noah: I bet you recycle, too?

Daryl: Naturally, doesn't everyone?

Noah: *Looking around.* I thought there was something different about this place. You know what it is? You don't have a single piece of plastic.

Daryl: Everything's natural. *Takes out the hamburger and hands it to him on a silver platter.*

Noah: *Whistling at the expensive plate.* Gee, even the plates and silverware are real silver. Aren't you afraid someone will walk off with this stuff?

Daryl: *Laughs.* They're welcome to it. They're just made of sand that has been transmuted into silver.

Noah: *Taking a big bite of his burger.* Transmuted?

Daryl: You know, atomic transmutation, the synthesis of expensive, unavailable chemical elements out of simpler, available ones.

Noah: Is that something like cold fusion?

Daryl: Yeah, it's simple. Here on the Island, we have mountains of sand. That silverware was formerly part of Jones Beach. It's basically worthless.

Noah: This sure is an unusual restaurant. *Changing the topic.* Do you have a radio? I'd like to catch the Mets.

Daryl: *Fiddles with an antenna.* Sure, but I don't think game time in Tokyo starts for another several hours.

Noah: *Aside.* Tokyo? I didn't know they played exhibition games in Japan during the summer. Hmm, probably offered them big bucks.

Daryl: *Searching the bandwave.* There's a pro basketball final, would that do?

Noah: I saw the championships last month. I'm not into reruns.

Daryl: No, this is coming live from the Moon.

Noah: An NBA final in July, from the Moon?

Daryl: Yeh, they have less gravity, so it makes for a more dynamic contest. The four-point bounce shot has revolutionized the game.

Noah: *Takes his last bite.* You're putting me on, Daryl. Thanks anyway, but I got a plane to catch. What's the damage? *Without waiting for an answer, he lays a $5 bill on the counter.* That ought to cover it. Keep the change.

Daryl: Thanks for the tip. But how do you want to pay for your meal?

Noah: Practically out the door. What, did I give you a single? *Fishes another $5 from his wallet and hands it to him.*

Daryl: Here's the total. *Hands him a bill.*

Noah: *Reads the check and thinks the decimal point is in the wrong place.* $15 for a hamburger! I knew Long Island real estate was overpriced, but this is robbery. *Hands him a couple fives and pointedly waits for the change.*

Daryl: I don't think you understand, Mister. You owe $15,000.

Noah: Where did you get that figure—out of thin air? *Sheepishly takes a silver spoon out of his coat jacket.* I thought you said this stuff was worthless. $15,000! All the silver in this place isn't worth that.

Daryl: Silver has nothing to do with it. The price for the hamburger is $15,000.

Noah: You're kidding. For $15,000 I could open my own franchise. *A few more forks and spoons tumble out of his pocket.*

Daryl: *Hands him the menu.* See, the price is printed right here on the menu.

Noah: Let me see that.
Sorghum burger, $3.15.

Tempeh burger $3.25.
Veggie burger $2.15.
Quinoa burger, $3.00.
Hamburger $15,000.

Daryl: Now do you believe me?

Noah: This is ridiculous. What did you serve me up, Brahma, the Bull which impregnated half the cows in Jersey? *Takes out his calculator.* Let's see, take a 1200-pound prize steer, at $15,000 a quarter-pound, that comes out to $72 million. A little high, don't you think, even by Long Island standards?

Daryl: Long Island?

Noah: Playing dumb, huh? I've heard of cab drivers charging $200 to take somebody from JFK to Manhattan, but this is the first time I've heard about a fast food joint set up by the airport to rip them off on the way. You have something going with my cabbie, don't you?

Daryl: Airport? The nearest airport is in the Catskills. And as for your driver out there, I never saw him in my life.

Noah: Yeh, well, I don't know what planet you live on, buddy, but I'm gonna report your scam to the authorities.

Daryl: By all means, please do so.

A patron eating in the far end of the restaurant notices the commotion and comes us.

Marty: Hey, Daryl, what's all the fuss? This guy stiffing you?

Noah: Who asked you?

Marty: *Shows him his badge.* Marty Richards, S.I.P.D. You gonna pay your bill or you gonna come with me?

Noah: This guy overcharged me for a hamburger. *Shows him the bill.* I think he got the decimal point off and won't admit it.

Marty: $15,000. Looks about right to me. My FEAT just caught a speeder on the way to get a cheeseburger at the place up the road for $17,500.

Noah: Your feet?

Marty: Sure, Fuel Efficiency Altitude Test. It's a device that shoots an infrared light at aeromobiles when they take off or land. A sensor picks up hydrogen emissions and alerts us to infractions. Where you been, buddy? Still driving an automobile?

Noah: What is this a conspiracy? You and Daryl here and Krishna out there are all in this together, aren't you? Unbelievable. *He starts to walk out.*

Marty: I wouldn't go out that door if I were you, Mister. *Takes out a lightstick and beams a light toward the door.*

Noah: What is this, *Star Trek*? *Sees that Marty is serious.* OK, I'll call your bluff. Arrest me. I'm not going to be railroaded by a pair of Klingons.

Krishna: *Coming in.* Sorry to disturb your chewing, Noah. But we'd better go if you want to make your flight.

Noah: *Aside.* How did I stumble into this acid factory? I almost forgot, I have a plane to catch. I'll lose a lot more than $15,000 if I don't make that meeting. *Turns to the others.* OK, guys, I give up. I'll pay you whatever you say.

Marty: That's more like it.

Noah: Do you take a credit card?

Daryl: Sure.

Noah: *To Krishna.* The dimwits. I'll call Visa from the airport and they'll close this place down in an hour.

Daryl: Sorry, sir, but this card has expired.

Spotlight focuses on a calendar on the wall. It's June 30, 2023.

Noah: Damn, Kathy must have forgotten to send in the renewal. *Fishes through his wallet and takes out several other cards.*

Daryl: *Holds them up and rubs them in the light.* Get a load of these, Marty.

Marty: *Bites the edge with his teeth.* Plastic, if I'm not mistaken.

Noah: Sure, what'd you expect—gold wafer?

Daryl: I'm sorry, sir, but we can't accept these.

Noah: What about a check? *Takes out his checkbook.*

Daryl: *Eyeballs the check.* Chase Manhattan. That was once a big bank in the region, wasn't it, Marty?

Marty: Yeh, they merged with that Saudi conglomerate, if I recall.

Noah: *Aside.* Chase was taken over? I didn't see a paper this afternoon or hear the news. Then anything's possible in today's world. *To the others.* Do you have CNN?

Daryl: CNN?

Noah: Yeh, Cable News Network.

Daryl: CNN, they were based in Atlanta, right?

Marty: Too bad about Atlanta—it sunk.

Noah: *Dumbfounded.* The overnight ratings killed CNN?

Daryl: Florida, Louisiana, the whole Gulf Coast went under.

Noah: You guys keep talking in riddles. Look, I gotta get to Seattle.

Daryl and Marty both shake their head at the same time.

Noah: Seattle, I suppose it sank too?

Daryl and Marty: Earthquake.

Noah: I'll have my accountant come over and settle up in the morning. Here, you can have my driver's license as collateral.

Marty: I'm afraid I'm gonna have to take you in.

Noah: I said I'd pay for it. Don't go gangbusters over one ditzy little hamburger.

Marty: *Reads him his rights.* Under article 2 of the S.I. penal code, I'm arresting you for grand theft for refusing to pay for your meal.
Holds up the credit cards. You are also being charged with possession of more than 2 ounces of plastic, a controlled substance, also a felony charge.
Finally, I am holding you under suspicion of having serum cholesterol level higher than 175 mg, a misdemeanor, unless of course it registers over 200 mg in which case it is a felony.
Anything you eat or drink can be used against you, you-have the right to an energy audit, and you are entitled to an environmental impact statement.

Noah: *Pointing to the cop's cap with S.I.P.D.* I'm afraid you're a little out of your jurisdiction, Staten Island. You can't arrest me.

Marty: S.I. stands for Short Island, not Staten Island.

Noah: You mean, as opposed to Long Island?

Daryl: Yeah, that's what they called it before The Warming.

Marty leads him off speechless.

Krishna: *Chants from the Gita.*
Heaven's gate swings open wide
for warriors who delight
to have a battle like this
come on them unsought.

Daryl: *Shaking his head. To Krishna.* Like I told him, he shoulda had the tempeh burger.

4

The next day in the courthouse in Northport. It is festooned with hanging and potted tropical plants. Shiva Deva enters and all rise. Noah, at the defendent's table, is surprised at how similar the Judge looks to Krishna Deva, the cab driver. Many of the other people present are dressed in T-shirts with pictures of colorful plants and animals.

Noah: Are you related by any chance to a cab driver from Bangalore and the Bronx?

Shiva: My chief residence is on Mt. Kailas in north India, and I have a second home in Benares.

Noah: Your hair is a little more matted and you carry a trident, but you have that same blue look.

Shiva: *Chants from the Gita.*
I know all creatures,
that have lived, or now exist,
and that one day shall be,
but, Noah, no one knows me.
Waves Noah to approach the bench and whispers. Don't be deceived by the heavy metal. It's me, Krishna. Shiva is my name on the bench.

Noah: How auspicious! What are you doing in judge's robes?

Shiva: I was a lawyer, remember?

Noah: How'd you get a judicial appointment so quick? Don't tell me, you're a spearcarrier for the Governor's reelection committee.

Shiva: I've held this office for a long time. The day I picked you up was my day off. I was moonlighting as a taxi driver. Parvati is always complaining about the household expenses, and our son, the elephant-headed Ganesh, eats us out of house and home.

Noah: *Sympathizes.* Tell me about it.

Shiva: *Looks at the file before him.* According to the healthcare authorities who examined you, you are suffering from GS.

Noah: GS?

Shiva: Greenhouse Syndrome. Like a hot house plant, the brain expands in the warm weather, causing something like sleeping sickness.

Noah: It feels like a hothouse in here.

Shiva: The last thirty years remain a complete blank to you. Thousands of people suffer from it. GS is a common defense in cases like this. If you plead it, I can get you a suspended sentence.

Noah: *Mulls it over and says to himself.* It's tempting, but I'll be damned if I pay through the nose for anything. What would Kathy and the kids think? *To the Judge.* Can't you get me off if I just tell the truth?

Shiva: Only you can deliver yourself, Noah. But I will be fair and impartial and do what I can.

Noah: Then I'll go for it. What about a lawyer to represent me?

Shiva: Lawyers and politicians were eliminated from the legal system a few years after The Warming. It was found that the fat and waste in government dropped by 40 percent. Everyone now represents himself.

Noah: What's this Warming everybody talks about?

The prosecutor, a slim but earnest man, rises.
Prosecutor: Enough chit chat, your honor. Can we get on with the proceedings? There's a warm front on its way and every-

one is anxious to get started.

Shiva: *Reviews the file on the case.* In the People vs. Wilson, the Court rules that two of the charges be dropped. Defendent's possession of a Class A controlled substance—plastic—proved to be lawfully owned by the corporations which issued the credit cards, not by the defendant. It says so right here. *Holds up the evidence.* Thus the plastic found on his person—a ballpoint pen and pocket comb—weighed less than 2 ounces, the minimum amount.

Noah gives the thumbs up sign.

Shiva: As for operating under high cholesterol, medical tests at the detention center showed the defendant had a serum reading of 179. Since the margin of error is plus or minus 4 points, I am going to give him the benefit of the doubt and have the record show that Mr. Wilson tested at 175, the legal limit. Since this is his first offense, he will be let off with a strong warning. *Shakes his trident at him menacingly.*

On the main charge, grand theft of goods and services worth over $5000, defendant has admitted to refusing to pay. However, he has challenged the arrest on the grounds that the fair market value of the hamburger he bought was unfairly priced. In a counterclaim, he contends that the said item was grossly overpriced and that the merchant defrauded him. Is that correct?

Noah: That is correct, your honor. It was a frame up from the start. Either the decimal point was off, or they served me up a quarterpound of some bovine superstud and charged accordingly.

Shiva: There have been sweeping changes over the last thirty years in medical and environmental law. I am going to allow this line of defense and place the burden of proof on the prosecution to show that the price of the hamburger was a legitimate one.

Prosecutor: Your honor, the state objects. The facts of the case are not in dispute. Mr. Wilson is on trial, not the restaurant or the laws of Adirondack.

Shiva: Call your first witness, Counselor.

Prosecutor: The state calls Albert Salisbury, M.D., director of Siegel-Kettering Memorial Hospital in New York. Dr. Salisbury is a specialist on toxic relationships and a recognized expert on health-care costs and serves on the governing board of directors of the New World Health Organization.

The witness goes up and hugs the Judge, the Prosecuter, and the defendent before taking his seat.

Noah: Point of order. What's a toxic relationship?

Dr. Salisbury: It's a poisonous relationship between two or more people. Like toxins in the environment, buried feelings, desires, and drives can pollute relations between parent and child, husband and wife, or employer and employee. Such a relationship needs to be detoxified.

Prosecutor: *Interrupting.* Could you please review the toxic relationship between meat consumption and medical costs.

Dr. Salisbury: Since the latter part of the 20th century, the relation between diet and degenerative disease has become well known. The principal cause of the modern epidemic of coronary heart disease, high blood pressure, cancer, diabetes, and many other chronic illnesses was the modern diet high in saturated fat, dietary cholesterol, simple sugar, refined flour, and other highly processed foods. The national insurance industry, you may recall, began to offer lower premiums to vegetarians and semi-vegetarians in the 1990s. The statistical rule of thumb was that red-meat, especially beef, could be held accountable for about 50 percent of direct and indirect medical costs. These include health insurance; direct medical costs such as doctors' visits, operations, medication, X-rays, etc.; Social Security and Medicaid; and state disability and unemployment.

Prosecuter: As Exhibit A, the state introduces into evidence the Heart Health Game introduced by the World Health Organization in the early 1990s. A simple board game designed for children, it features a large heart around which players move markers, throw dice, and compete to reach the goal of a healthy heart. Along the way, as in Monopoly, they land on specially designated squares in which they pick cards. For example, if a child lands on a Diet Square, a typical heart-shaped card reads, "'I like junk food. What's wrong with a burger or chips?' Boo! Go back 2 squares. Frequently the meat drips with saturated fats—the bad fat—and the chips are fried in saturated oil. Read aloud from paragraph 4 of the Guide to Healthy Living." Paragraph 4 reads: "There are different kinds of fat: good and bad. Unsaturated fat, which is mainly liquid from plants, is good. Saturated fat, usually solid, is bad. Bad 'sat fats' come mainly from animals, and dairy products, where the fat content has not been reduced.'" In short, it was well established among the world's highest medical and healthcare agencies by this time that meat and dairy food, especially hamburger, were harmful, not only to people at high risk for degenerative disease, but also to children and teens. By the beginning of the century, it was well established that the foundation of heart disease, cancer, and other chronic ills began in infancy and childhood, and the time to prevent them was early in life, rather than later after they had manifested. In 1990s dollars, Dr. Salisbury, what was the annual total of direct and indirect medical costs?

Dr. Salisbury: By the end of the decade roughly $2 trillion. Average per capita consumption of hamburger at that time was 128 quarter-pound patties. Considering that about 10 percent of the population was completely vegetarian and another 10 percent semi-vegetarian, eating fish and seafood but rarely meat, the average per capita consumption on the part of those who ate meat was more like 156 hamburgers or three per week. Actually, the exact amounts were 1.7 hamburgers for those under 7, 6.2 for children 7 to 13, and 5.2 for persons 13 to 30. After that it began to decline. For statistical purposes, we figure that this represented approximately 50% of an individual's total meat consumption. Dividing $1 trillion—or the amount of direct and indirect medical costs attributed to meat-eating—by a meat-eating population of then about 200,000,000, we get $4000 per capita. Of this, $2000 is charged to hamburgers. Dividing by 156, we get about $13 per hamburger. That is the figure that is now routinely used in insurance claim cases in this state.

Noah: *Obviously relieved at the small amount. In an aside to the*

Judge. $13 bucks, pretty small potatoes.

Prosecuter: I understand that in addition, doctor, there are morbidity costs, i.e., lost productivity as a result of premature death.

Noah's face drops.

Dr. Salisbury: You will recall that these were first calculated in the class action suits against the tobacco industry in the late 1990s, followed by the meat and poultry industries. In Rifkin vs. the National Cattleman's Association, the Supreme Court upheld an award to the widow of a 56-year-old man who had died of a heart attack and who claimed that a life of eating hamburgers had killed her husband. Following testimony by the Dietitian-General, the court held that his life was shortened by at least 30 years and awarded him $3 million. Of course, later after the precedent was set, awards were reduced, to an average of $35,000 per year. Given an individual during that era typically ate 3840 hamburgers before dying of a degenerative disease, each hamburger also costs $273 in lost earnings.

Noah: *A little taken aback by this higher figure.* Just one question, Dr. Salisbury. The list you submitted includes not only heart disease and cancer, but many other conditions. *Reads from fact sheet.* I see here infertility and impotency. Do your figures includes these as well? And if so, how are these connected with beef consumption?

Dr. Salisbury: The relation between diet and reproductive disorders became well established in the first decade of the current century as the infertility rate climbed from 35 percent in the 1990s to nearly 50 percent. Scientists found that fat and cholesterol accumulated in the Fallopian tubes preventing conception, and when the woman was put on a low-fat, high-fiber diet, fertility usually returned. Similarly, in the case of impotence, arteriosclerosis in the penis was found to be the chief cause of inability to perform. When the diet was changed and grain- and vegetable-quality foods substituted for meat and dairy, the frequency of this disorder almost vanished.

Noah: *To the Judge.* Well, I guess that little piece of information is worth $273 to my future love life. *To the court.* Dr. Salisbury, are you any relation to the Lord Salisbury, the famous British jurist?

Dr. Salisbury: *Torn.* I believe he is a distant cousin, several times removed.

Noah: Could you tell the court what Lord Salisbury is best remembered for?

Dr. Salisbury: He is known as the originator of the Salisbury Steak.

Noah: And isn't it fair to say that you have a toxic relationship with your cousin and that his carnivorous past colors your whole analysis?

Prosecutor: Objection, this is pure conjecture on the part of the defendent.

Noah: *Triumphantly.* Question withdrawn.

Doctor Salisbury steps down, turns a cold shoulder to Noah, and exits.

Prosecutor: The State calls Sarah Dunlap.

The spotlight focuses on the telecom, a large life-size television-computer screen, situated in the front of the court. A young girl with crutches appears and is sworn in.

Prosecutor: Please tell the people here your name and story.

Sara: My name is Sara. I'm ten years old. I live with my family and go to school in Corn Silk, Nebraska. When I was little, I used to play in the stream that runs behind our electronic cottage. I was hoping to find a minnow there. I had never seen a fish before. But when I started to break out in rashes and my arms and neck started to swell, doctors found I had lymphoma. They said it was caused by chemicals in fertilizers that had gotten into the water.

Prosecutor: What were the chemicals used for?

Sara: They were used for cattle-raising. There used to be a lot of beef and dairy cattle in Mound before The Warming. They were fed with antibiotics and hormones to fatten them. And the feed was all grown with these poisons.

Prosecutor: Are there any other children like yourself in your area?

Sarah: Well, there's Ned, he's in the second grade, and he has leukemia. There's Robin, she's two years older than me, and has a kidney tumor. And this cute little baby at church, Russell, he has a brain tumor.

Prosecutor: Thank you Sara. Let the record show that the incidence of childhood cancer in the bioregion of the Ogalla Aquifier, Mound's largest water table, stretching from the Hotlands in South Dakota to the Great Midwest Desert in Kansas, is five times the national average. According to the National Research Council, America's highest scientific panel, in 1987, insecticides accounting for 30 percent, herbicides accounting for 50 percent, and fungicides accounting for 90 percent of all agricultural use were found to cause tumors in laboratory studies. Furthermore, according to a panel of the A.A.A.S., as early as 1981 it was reported that production of animal foods used nearly 80 percent of all piped water in the United States, and was chiefly responsible for pollution of two-thirds of U.S. basins and for generating over half of the pollution burden entering the nation's lakes and streams. As *Newsweek*, a predecessor to *Weatherweek*, put it, "The water that goes into a thousand-pound steer would float a destroyer." Animal waste, for example, caused algae in streams and riverbeds to overfertilize, depleted oxygen, and suffocated aquatic systems. The average American eating animal food at that time used 608,000 gallons of water per year. That was about ten times the amount of water used by the average person on the planet eating whole grains and vegetables.

While no one can put a price on little Sara's suffering, we can look at this as a typical example of the effects of modern chemical farming, particularly beef and dairy production, on the world's water supply. In the 1990s, the U.S. government was subsidizing water projects in the western part of the country to the tune of $2.2 billion annually. Since the establishment of the Global Pure Water Authority in the early part of this century, the cost of cleaning the planet's rivers, streams, lakes, and coastal waterways has exceeded $10.8 trillion. Based on the 80 percent figure noted above, the cost of water pollution per hamburger consumed in the years B.S. comes to $214.

Noah: B.S.?

Prosecutor: Before the Summit. The Earth Summit in Rio in 1992. *Snickers.* Of course, that's not an official designation on the New World Calendar. But a lot of people refer to the era before The Warming by those initials.

Noah: *Getting up and addressing the telecom.* Sara, I truly sympathize with you and hope that you make a complete recovery. You remind me of my little girl. You mentioned that your family had an electronic cottage. *Putting her at ease.* What do you study in school?

Sara: The four R's—renovating, restoring, renewing, and recycling.

Noah: What do your Mommy and Daddy do?

Prosecutor: Objection, your honor. The occupation and lifestyle of Sara's family is immaterial to this proceeding.

Noah: Your honor, electronic cottage suggests a computerized environment. The health effects of such an environment may offer an alternative explanation for her illness.

Shiva: Sustained. Sara, please answer the question.

Sara: Daddy works on a computer. I don't have a Mommy. Just after teaching me how to swim, she died of breast cancer.

Noah: *Taken aback with mixed emotions.* I'm very sorry, Sara. But let the record show that household exposure to extremely low frequency radiation may be the source of her illness. *Triumphantly.* I have no further questions.

Prosecutor: Let the record show that Mr. Dunlap worked as a dairy farmer for twenty years. After suffering a heart attack and being unable to work the farm, he got a job doing promotion for the Nebraska Livestock Board. He rose to assistant manager for the "Beef Is Real Food for Real People" campaign.

Noah: *Aside.* Wouldn't you know it, they picked someone whose disability was tied to the beef industry. No lawyers, my eye. They all became prosecutors and judges.

Prosecutor: Let it be stated that EMF, artificial electromagnetic fields, have been severely curtailed in the last generation, especially in food processing, cooking, and home appliance use. Today, Sara's father works for the Nebraska Soy Cooperative and heads up the "Tofu Is Healthy Food for Healthy People" campaign.

Noah scowls.

Prosecutor: If it please the court, the State is prepared to bring to the stand other witnesses to buttress the relation between cattle raising and water pollution.

Shiva: *Looks at list of other potential witnesses and assumes a yogic posture with one knee pulled up beneath him.* I have all the time in the world, Noah, how about you? Would you like to hear their testimony?

Noah: *Taken aback.* No, I don't think that will be necessary. I'd just as soon speed up this trial. I have to get back home. We have a barbe——barbershop quarter rehearsal on Saturday.

Shiva: The court will take a short yoga break. *Leans over toward Noah in the Grasshopper pose.* Would you care to stretch or have some carrot juice?

Noah: Just a Coke, thanks.

Shiva: Whistling the theme song from *Alice's Restaurant*:
"You can get anything you want,
From Alice's restaurant . . . "

Maya, the judge's assistant, brings in a Coke.

Judge: I'd look at the bill first this time.

Noah: *Practically faints at the bill.* On second thought, I'll have the carrot juice.

Maya takes away the Coke unopened.

Shiva: *Chants from the Gita.*
Renouncing the fruits of action,
the person of discipline attains perfect peace;
the person without discipline is entangled,
attached to the fruits of their desire.

Noah: Thanks, I owe you one.

Shiva: Don't mention it.

Noah: *Walks over to the telecom.* This gizmo is pretty interesting.

Shiva: It allows us to take testimony from around the world. It also serves as an interactive information and entertainment center, something like television in the old days. *Touches the panel at the side of the screen and a series of numbers flash on.* This shows the subject's blood pressure, cholesterol level, heartbeat, respiratory rate, and other key metabolic indicators. It helps in the evaluation of their condition and testimony.

Noah: *Looking at the dials on the monitor.* What other channels do you receive?

Shiva: Of course, there's ENN—Earth Network News. Most of the channels are devoted to interactive cultural programming—folklore, mythology, song and dance, art and architecture, and other traditional arts and sciences from around the world. But, as you might imagine, the most popular channel is the Weather Channel. Syndicated reruns of earthquakes, floods, volcanos, and other disasters are extremely popular. *Sighs.* Human nature! *To Noah.* Then there are the biodegradable soaps—*As the World Burns, One Life to Give, Young, Hot, and Restless.*

Noah: *Going over to the window to cool off and holding his nose.* The air here really hasn't changed all that much in 30 years. What's that stench coming in from the sea?

Shiva: The air and sea now are pretty clean. What you smell is cow dung.

Noah: *Looking down.* Holy cow! There's a huge bull down there doubled parked in your parking spot.

Shiva: That's Nandi, my mount.

Noah: You drive a bullock cart? The world really has gone back to the dark ages.

Shiva: *Au contraire,* he's state of the art. Not only does he take me where I need to go at warp speed, but his droppings can be used for fuel and fodder. *Chants from the Gita.*
I am the thunderbolt among divine weapons,
I am the cleansing wind,
Among rivers, I am the swift flowing Ganges.
Among cattle, the magical wish-granting cow.

Noah: *Aside.* Me thinks there are grounds here for a mistrial beyond the Judge's obvious Multiple Personality Disorder. Should Krishna, Shiva, or what's his face rules against me, I can have him disqualified for being prejudiced against beef and hamburgers because of the family cow. *Rubs his hands together gleefully.*

Shiva: The court will resume its deliberations.

Prosecutor: The state calls Ibraham Salim, the celebrated film maker.

A distinguished middle-aged man, walking with a slight limp, appears on the telecom from Karachi.

Salim: My name is Ibraham Salim. I was born and raised in Pakistan. I grew up in a small village called Kasan. Like my grandfather and his father before him, my father tilled the ancestral field, supplying our family with rice and wheat, lentils and fresh vegetables. When I was still a boy, a multinational came to our region and started buying up the small farms in order to raise cattle. These brought a much greater profit. But Father wouldn't sell, saying he would continue in the old way. Eventually, through corrupt local officials, our land was confiscated, Father was beaten, and we were forced off our farm.

We went to Karachi where we had a distant relative, but Father couldn't find work. We lived on the street and in the slums for several years, until Father died of tuberculosis. Two of my younger brothers died of diarrhea from infant formula and other foods we received from a local charity. I survived by my wits, selling bootleg videos and cassettes. Eventually I was able to get an education, find work in the communications ministry making documentaries, and find a home for my mother and sisters.

Prosecutor: Let the record show that since 1492 the modern cattle culture has spread across the world, overturning traditional cultures and ways of living that have existed for thousands of years. There are hundreds of millions of families like Salim's that have been uprooted from their traditional farms and villages. Seeking food and employment, they have flocked into urban cities, creating vast slums and a vicious spiral of hunger, poverty, disease, and crime. In this atmosphere, women are abused and birth rates soar out of control, contributing to further destitution. As early as 1970, Frances Moore Lappé showed that there was more than enough food to feed all the world's people. The problem was that most of it was going to feed cattle. Nutritionists determined that it took roughly 40 times as much energy to produce one pound of beef as it did to produce one pound of grain. In the San Paolo Declaration, you will recall, this multiplication factor of 40 was used by the New World Government in calculating the amount of money which the developed countries owed to developing countries for past injustices. Later the New World Court assessed the rich meat-eating countries triple damages as a legacy of centuries-old political, economic, and social oppression and set up a Superfund for Cultural Survival. Thus, the cost of animal protein went up 120 times (i.e. 40 times 3 times $2/pound of beef), adding another $240 to the price of hamburger.

Noah: Your honor, I object to being held responsible for the sins of Columbus, Cortez, Chiquita Banana, and Nestle's.

Shiva: *Waves Noah to the bench.* Be thankful the prosecutor didn't bring up the issue of slavery.

Noah: Slavery?

Shiva: Slavery was fueled for three centuries by the sugar industry. About twenty years ago, in the matter of Jackson vs. Domino's *et al.* the entire North American food industry—or at least the 90 percent of it which used sugar in some capacity—was almost taken over. The Rainbow Coalition contended that it should assume control over the nation's supermarkets because of this past legacy of oppression, growing medical evidence linking crime, violence, and other antisocial behavior with sugar and fast food consumption, and its successful track record in community food programs beginning with Operation Breadbasket. Only Chief Justice Thomas's vote breaking a 4-4 deadlock averted this from happening.

Noah: Run, Jesse, run.

Shiva: As consolation, Rev. Jackson's group received Coca-Cola Bottling Company. After replacing sugar and kola nuts—an African product that was overcultivated and damaging to the native environment—with better quality ingredients, Coke was renamed Health-Cola.

A youthful looking Chinese man in white shirt and glasses appears on the telecom and is sworn in.

Prosecutor: The State calls Li Wei, director of the Salt Plum Blossom Health Cooperative in Suchou, China.

Prosecutor: Could you tell us about the nature of your work and findings?

Le Wei: I administer a large drug and alcohol rehabilitation center in South China. In the last twenty-five years, thousands of former addicts and substance abusers have successfully completed treatment. This included many refugees from Hong Kong after The Sinking.

Noah: Your honor, this witness is not germaine. What possible relevance has drug and alcohol treatment to do with the price of hamburger?

Shiva: Overruled. I will grant the state some *leeway* to make its point. Continue, counselor.

Prosecutor: Dr. Li Wei, could you tell us what is the chief cause of substance abuse?

Li Wei: Formerly, it was thought it resulted from moral failing, lack of religious instruction, breakdown of the family, job stress, and other social-psychological factors. However, various approaches to correct these failed. In the last generation, it has become clear that drug addition and alcoholism are essentially a biological problem.

According to traditional Oriental medicine and philosophy, all foods and beverages, plants and animals, and other things can be classified into yin and yang. Yin or earth's force is the force of expansion. It creates relaxation, growth, diffusion, passivity. Yang or heaven's force is the force of contraction. It creates tightness, compactness, gathering, activity. The most balanced foods for daily consumption—combining an ideal balance of yin and yang—are whole grains and vegetables, beans and seaweeds.

Animal foods are classified as extremely yang. They give strong energy and vitality, but make the body tight, hard, hot, rigid. Naturally, to make balance, people eating animal food are attracted to extreme yin in the form of sugar and sweets, alcohol, drugs, and other substances that cool down and relax the body.

The principal cause of drug addition and alcoholism then is longtime past consumption of meat, poultry, eggs, dairy food, and other predominantly animal products. These problems cannot be cured by prohibition or making drugs illegal as was tried in the last century. However, they can easily be solved by eliminating the craving for extreme yin. To do that, you need to substantially cut back on yang animal food consumption.

In our clinic, we have had remarkable success by putting substance abusers on a balanced diet, essentially the same kind of high-fiber, low-fat, fresh food diet that helped eliminate heart disease, cancer, AIDS, and other degenerative diseases.

Prosecutor: Let the record show that the annual cost of alcohol and drug abuse, in medical and social costs, reached the hundreds of billions of dollars annually. Demographers have shown a clearcut pattern of drug and alcohol use following the spread of fast food around the planet. In the last several years, MAD—Mothers Against Dairy—and other pro-family organizations waged a successful effort to add an alcohol and drug rehabilitation surcharge to the cost of animal food. This surcharge, amounting to 700 percent, was based on the traditional ratio of 1:7. In other words, it takes 7 parts yin to balance 1 part yang. Using $2 as the baseline cost of a hamburger in the B.S. era adds $14 to the cost of a hamburger.

Noah: Your honor, I object. Le Wei's testimony is all pseudoscience, Oriental mumbo-jumbo. Yin and yang are no more scientific than astrology or fad diets. You can't convince me that the Mafia or Medallin drug traffickers are going to reform by eating tofu and brown rice.

Prosecutor: Your honor, that is exactly what the State intends to prove.

Shiva: *Chants from the Gita.*
He who perceives me in everything
and sees everything in me
will find the unity of life;
wherever he is, he remains in me.
Zaps the telecom with his trident like a TV remote. Proceed.

Noah: *Aside.* I need a stiff drink.

A burly Spaniard with a long, drooping mustache and scar across his chin approaches the witness chair and is sworn in.

Prosecutor: The State calls Carlos Martinique. Please tell us about your background and present activities.

Carlos Martinique: My name is Carlos Martinique, better known in my younger days as "Big Burrito." I grew up in Barcelona, emigrated to Columbia, and became a cocaine kingpin. I had a fleet of private jets, bank accounts—make that, banks—in a dozen countries, mistresses galore, and three prime ministers at my beck and call. My syndicate was better armed than most of the countries in Latin America. In fact, we sold our surplus weapons to the U.S. Army. However, despite all this wealth, power, and influence, I was eventually brought to trial. My wife, a prime minister, and one of the bankers sold me out to a competitor. Before I knew it I was residing in a concrete bungalow.

Prosecutor: What happened in prison?

Carlos Martinique: Prison life was rough, and many prisoners didn't survive. There were constant fights. Often I ended up in solitary. I was a battler, and had been most of my life. I had always loved bull fights. I identified with the bull. I'd see red whenever anyone provoked me and charge ahead regardless of the consequences.

One day I got to talking with a fellow named Senor Antonio. He was the only prisoner I couldn't bully—or bribe. He was always pleasant and never took offense at any of my taunts. He always had everything under control. I finally broke down and asked him how me managed to stay so cool. He said that the secret was proper food. He gave me some brown rice and tofu to eat. He showed me some breathing exercises and gave me some books by Michio Kushi to read.

Now I hadn't eaten rice and beans since I left the barrios as a kid. I'd always liked beef, eggs, pork, you know, the prime cuts. To tell you the truth, I still had a steady supply in prison because of my past connections. They didn't call me "Big Burrito" because of soybeans in my taco.

Well, prison changes your perspective. I started eating with Antonio and started feeling great. Pretty soon, I was cooking for myself. Of course, chopping vegetables was hard without a knife. But I got by. In a year, I had lost 35 pounds, my mood swings disappeared, and I was giving shiatsu massage to the other inmates. The guards and prison administrators were amazed at my transformation. Of course, at first a lot of them thought it was a trick, but eventually they became convinced. In three years, I was declared rehabilitated and released. In Medallin, I started a vegetarian restaurant. My wife came back to me. I hired the banker and ex-prime minister who had sold me out as dishwashers, and my brother, "Little Burrito," set up a seitan factory. Now we have a chain of slow-food restaurants throughout Central and Latin America. They now call me "Big Tofu."

Noah: Your honor, I don't care how many sprouts he's sliced. I'd still hate to meet up with this guy in a dark pantry.

Prosecutor: Let the record show that the relation between crime and diet is now universally accepted. As early as the 1970s, corrections officials in Cayahoga County, Ohio, and Chesapeake, Virginia, introduced natural foods into the penal system. One study, for example, observed a 45 percent reduction in aggressive and antisocial behavior when sugar was cut out of the diet of youthful offenders. The recidivism rate dropped to less than 10 percent. Medically, the condition underlying most crime—as in Carlos's case—is hypoglycemia, or chronic low blood sugar. This results from a combination of eating strong animal foods and sugar, sweets, fruit, alcohol, and the like. Hyperactive behavior, lower SAT scores, and general bullying and cowing—or intimidating behavior—are all typical of a community in which beef is the principal food. The estimated costs of crime to society are in the hundreds of billions every year. The New World Court has commonly held that the social costs of products, services, and antisocial behavior as a rule extend three generations. On this basis, the $2 base cost per hamburger times 90 years, we add $180 to the price of a hamburger, bringing the total for substance abuse and crime-related costs to $194.

Noah: Your honor, I can't believe the Twinkie's defense has been accepted into law. In my era, this was laughed out of court.

Shiva: *Chants from the Gita.*
In your era, men and women of delusion
could not fathom
activity and rest;
there existed no clarity,
no balance, no insight or understanding in them.

The next witness, a woman with big hips appears on the telecom and is sworn in.

Noah: *Aside.* Uh, oh—Venus of Willendorf is on deck. They're going to sock it to me for the oppression of women since the Stone Age.

Prosecutor: The State calls Rebecca Mir.

Rebecca: My name is Rebbeca Mir. I was born in Israel and grew up on a kibbutz. When I was seventeen, I joined the Army and rose to captain. I was stationed in Lebanon for several years, combatting antiterrorist activity. It was a very dirty campaign, and it was hard to tell the terrorists from ordinary people. A lot of innocents were caught in the middle.

One day our forces were out on patrol and came to part of the no man's territory dividing the Christians and Moslems. Ordinarily this is the most dangerous zone, because both sides claimed the land and friction was high. But this part of Beirut was different. The Moslems and Christians were still friends. The children were playing together, the parents were trading, religious worship was going on side by side. Nobody could understand what was going on here.

I investigated and discovered that things had begun to change a few years earlier when people started to make traditional whole grain bread. For many years, they had been eating white, refined bread and buying food imported from France and Greece. But then this little girl had been healed of cancer on a simple macrobiotic diet, and people started making the bread again the way their grandparents used to. They called it Wise Bread because it made you healthy, wealthy, and wise. A community bakery was set up, giving people jobs, and later with the money they started planting grains and vegetables and set up an agricultural cooperative. The level of tension and distrust just melted away—"like tumors in an individual," as one of the organizers told me.

Later, I returned to Israel and interested my kibbutz in organic farming. They had long since stopped growing foods like this in favor of livestock, citrus fruit, and other cash crops. The change was amazing. Pretty soon Arab and Jewish settlers who had been threatening each other were working side by side. Everybody's health improved, and the whole area grew more peaceful. At the present time, I am a bioregional operations director for the Earth Corps and have been involved in environmental peace-keeping missions in the Amazon, the Yangtze

River Delta, and the Caribbean coral reefs.

Prosecutor: Let the record show that the relation between diet and war has been exhaustively studied. In the Far East, the ideograms for peace were "grain" and "mouth." Ancient people intuitively knew that by eating whole grains, society naturally became peaceful. In ancient India, the word for *war* was "desire for cows." In the last century, Professor Quincy Wright, an adviser to the U.S. War Department at the Nuremburg Tribunal, published his magnum opus, *A Study of War*, in which he concluded that the wars of modern civilization were unnatural and linked to animal food consumption. Conversely, he noted that "the trend of evolution has been toward symbiotic relations and perhaps toward vegetarian diet." Conservatively, the estimated cost of wars in the 20th century stretch into the trillions of dollars and hundreds of millions of casualties. As late as 1990, when the Cold War was over, annual arms expenditures reached $980 billion a year. Adding this to an estimated $10 trillion in worldwide war-related costs per year, the social costs of each hamburger consumed come to $988.

Noah: *To the Judge.* At least it wasn't reparations for women's lib. *To the court.* I have no questions of the witness at this time. I would only ask the court to recall that Hitler was a vegetarian.

Prosecutor: *Indignantly.* He was a chocoholic, an amphetamine addict, and hypoglycemic. I submit, your honor, that the discharge of past animal food was responsible for Hitler's conduct.

Shiva: Both the defense and prosecution are out of order. We are not here to relive and assess blame for World War II. *Stamps his trident and the monsoon rains start to fall outside.* The court is adjourned until tomorrow morning.

Noah: *Amazed.* Now how'd he do that?

5

The next morning, the court resumes to hear testimony on the environment. A striking red-headed woman appears on the telecom and is sworn in.

Prosecutor: The State calls Ellen Schwartz.

Ellen Schwartz: My name is Ellen Schwartz. I run an aeromobile assembly plant in Provo, Utah, in the bioregion of Mesa. Before that I was a pilot in the Desert Storm operation in Iraq and forewoman at G.M.—General Mitsubishi in Dai Troit—in the light equipment division.

Noah: Your honor, what do tanks and batmobiles have to do with the price of hamburger?

Shiva: *Raises his trident in irritation.* Objection overruled. The witness may continue.

Ellen Schwartz: At G.M., I was involved in the manufacture of tractors, irrigation tank trucks, refrigerator cars, and other vehicles used in modern agriculture and food delivery.

Prosecutor: What percentage of the industrial manufacturing base of this country was involved in such work?

Ellen Schwartz: At its peak, production, processing, and preparation of animal foods consumed 14 to 17 percent of America's national energy budget.

Prosecutor: Let the record show that this was roughly equivalent to the fuel needed to power all the automobiles in the nation at that time and more than twice the energy supplied by all the nuclear power plants in operation.

Noah: I don't see what transportation has to do with anything?

Prosecutor: Trips to the fast food chain or the supermarket for a bottle of milk or ground beef accounted for over a third of all automobile use before The Warming. Hundreds of times more calories in fossil fuel energy were expended than returned in the food purchased. Please continue, Captain Schwartz.

Ellen Schwartz: The processing and packaging of animal foods used large amounts of strategically important and critically scarce raw materials including aluminum, copper, iron and steel, tin, zinc, potassium, rubber, wood, and petroleum products. The front office once sent me undercover to Zimbabwe to wine and dine some chieftain who controlled the world's market in chromium.

Noah: What happened?

Ellen Schwartz: He offered to make me his third best wife. It was tempting, but I could never leave Harry. I gave him $20 million in U.S.D.A. surplus food credits, an air-conditioned minivan, and backstage tickets to a Michael Jackson concert. I came home with 10 tons of heavy metal.

Noah presses the dials on the telecom and her blood pressure numbers flash on the screen and start to climb up, challenging her veracity.

Prosecutor: *Flustered.* Let the record show that the direct industrial costs related to animal food production and packaging add substantially to the cost of a hamburger. In that era, industry was powered primarily by fossil fuels, especially petroleum. When formulating the Carbon Tax several decades ago, economists noted that the average American used the equivalent of about 1 gallon of gasoline a day for the preparation and packaging of meat, poultry, eggs, and dairy food. According to the head of the Greenhouse Crisis Foundation, for a typical family of four, the annual amount of hamburger and other animal food consumed released the average equivalent of 5 times more carbon dioxide into the atmosphere than the family car. The market price of oil in that era was roughly $1.00 to $1.35 a gallon. However, as the Valdez Principles and subsequent international accords proved, the true price of oil to society and the environment needed to be multiplied many times over. Beyond the real costs of irreplaceable fossil fuels and mineral-depletion, the cost in oil spills, air pollution, gas emissions, and environmental disasters occasioned by geopolitical conflicts and wars over petroleum such as the Persian Gulf War in 1991 add another $1,483 to the price of hamburger. This is based on the New World Court's precedent of generally assessing environment costs over the course of the next seven generations.

Noah: No questions, your honor, except to note that at home my wife has a chromium-lined wok for making stir-fried veggies. Also, I don't know what percentage of whole wheat bread in the health food stores is still kneaded and sliced by hand, but I would guess it's lower than Dwight Gooden's batting average.

An elderly man with Einstein-like hair appears on the telecom and takes the stand.

Prosecutor: The state calls Professor Yuri Volshoya.

Yuri Volshoya: My name is Yuri Volshoya. I run the bioreactor in Kiev. Before that I was a nuclear scientist. As a young man, I participated in the clean up of Chernobyl, following the nuclear accident there in 1986.

Prosecutor: Could you tell us, Professor Volshoya, what was the purpose of the nuclear reactor at Chernobyl? We know it was a power plant, but exactly what was the power generated used for?

Yuri Volshoya: Of course, the electricity generated was used for industry, transportation, communications, and other segments of society. But the biggest use was for agriculture, especially irrigation for pasture land. As you know, the Soviet Union embarked on an ambitious modernization program after the Second World War. Agriculture, the foundation of our economy, was based on farming. But during this period, farming changed from producing rye, barley, oats, buckwheat, and other traditional foods to producing livestock. Our leaders wanted to catch up with the West and provide a comparable amount of animal protein as in America and Britain. The commissars had their own well stocked stores, but they knew putting meat on the table for the ordinary family was the key to maintaining their power. In the USSR, per capita meat consumption tripled between 1950 and 1990.

Noah: What about the big wheat deals of the 1970s and 1980s? If they ate so much meat, why didn't they import hogs or steers?

Yuri Volshoya: The wheat deals brought in millions of metric tons of grain from the American Midwest, three-quarters of which went to provide fodder for livestock. By the late 1980s and early 1990s, Russia had the most chemically-intensive agriculture in the world, surpassing the U.S. in artificial fertilizer and pesticide use. Ukraine and Belarus, the areas around Chernobyl, once known as the Breadbasket of the Soviet Union, became the livestock and poultry capital. Chicken Kiev—a famous dish—brought in badly needed tourist dollars. The same is true in other regions. The Aral Sea shrunk by 66 percent in volume and 40 percent in area since 1960 when water was diverted to agricultural irrigation. This caused severe soil salination and acidification, and the Aral became known as the "Salty Sea of Death." Lake Baikal in Siberia, the Amu Dar'ya River (the "Sewer of Central Asia"), and other major natural resources were also severely polluted. Of course, the situation is reversed today. The Russian Federation is exporting grain to the arid American Midwest.

Prosecutor: Let the record show that this pattern was typical, not only in Russia, but in many Eastern bloc countries. In this country, the same pattern emerged, though to a lesser extent. The nuclear plant in Seabrook, N.H., for example, generated power to fuel dairy farmers in Vermont as well as high-tech computer workers in Nashua and along Boston's Route 128. The costs to date of the worldwide nuclear clean-up have exceeded $10 trillion over the last thirty years. Despite great strides in bioreactors, these expenditures will extend into the foreseeable future. This includes direct and indirect medical expenses for the 50 to 250 million people directly exposed to nuclear radiation, death benefits for the approximately 3 million who died from radiation-related cancers, the decommisioning of over 400 nuclear plants, storage and transportation of 450,000 tons of irradiated fuel and high level nuclear waste, and clean up of mines, lakes, rivers, testing grounds, and other areas contaminated by nuclear energy. Until a permanent solution is found, nuclear waste is presently being entombed in the

Pentagon in Washington, D.C., the CIA headquarters in McLean, Virginia, and other former military and intelligence sites. A main component of this waste, Plutonium-239, remains dangerous for 360,000 years, so suffice it to say that future generations will be paying for the upkeep, replacement, and storage of this modern mountain of contamination for many generations. The most modest estimates of the cost of this storage, plus the indemnity for the millions already adversely affected by nuclear energy, comes to $5090 for every hamburger consumed since 1992.

Noah: Pardon my ignorance, but what is a bioreactor?

Yuri Volshaya: A bioreactor is a big tank that treats toxic wastes with living microorganisms. The principle was first established in the early 1990s when bacteria were used experimentally to help clean up the *Mega Borg* oil spill in the Gulf of Mexico.

Noah: There are organisms that eat oil?

Yuri Volshoya: And other toxic wastes. Eventually we hope to find one that is able to dine on uranium, strontium, and other radioactive particles.

Dr. Volshoya takes something out of his briefcase and hands it to Noah.

Noah: *Recoils.* What's this—radioactive clay?

Yuri Volshoya: *Laughs.* No, it's a kilo of freeze dried bacteria.

Noah: Looks just like pancake batter to me.

Yuri Volshoya: Of course, it needs to be mixed with water to become activated. It will eat a hundred times its weight in heavy metals.

Noah: *Aside.* This is a million-dollar idea. I can see the storyboards: "Get Mop and Glow," "Waste Not, Want Not," "Melt Down the Toxic Waste in Your Kitchen with New Improved Meltdown." *To the court.* What's the half-life—I mean shelf life—of this bacteria batter?

Yuri Volshoya: About a year. Then it begins to go stale.

Shiva: *Sarcasticly chants from the Gita.*
When he sees the oneness
existing in different creatures
and how they expand from unity,
he profits by the infinite spirit.

Noah: Did you use this stuff to protect you in Chernobyl?

Yuri Volshoya: No, it wasn't developed until later. However, after the clean up, I ate a lot of miso, seaweed, and other foods that are protective against nuclear radiation.

Noah: *Pressing the telecom dials and checking out the radioactive content of his bones.* Hm, telling the truth.

Shiva: We're getting off the subject, amigos. Let's move on with the cross-examination.

Noah: Do you think, Professor, that the nuclear arms race and the Cold War were primarily responsible for the development and spread of atomic energy? Wasn't everything else a by-product?

Yuri Volshoya: Certainly.

Noah: And isn't it true that many of the large agricultural projects in the Soviet era were for show, for either domestic or international consumption?

Yuri Volshoya: Yes, most definitely. Many were a standing joke, and compared to Potemkin Villages—hastily arranged to impress visiting dignitaries or comrades from Moscow how progressive the region was.

Noah: *Triumphantly.* No further questions. *Aside.* I should have been on *Miami Vice* or *L.A. Law*.

A stately man in African robes and turban appears on the telecom and is sworn in.

Prosecutor: The State calls Mwalimu Tombo.

Mwalimu Tombo: My name is Mwalimu Tombo. I appear before you today from the Abode of Sands. It wasn't always this way. In my youth, my home was known as the Land of Green Meadows. There were endless fields of millet and sorghum, sparkling waters, and billowing clouds. But after the cattle came and trampled the land, the crops dried up. The ground became impermeable to rain, carrying away the topsoil and transforming streambeds into deep gullies. Years of hunger and starvation followed the droughts. There were no clouds, no rain. I was separated from my family in the refugee camps. Today I work for the International Green Cross and Crescent, farming and gardening, planting tree breaks, and digging wells to take back the desert. We have sown grains and vegetables in clay pellets that are dropped from airplanes. The pellets protect the seeds in the arid environment, and eventually they germinate when enough moisture is collected. This is part of the New World Government's campaign to "Sow Seeds, Not Bombs." We have also been especially successful with the neem tree.

Shiva: It is native to India, isn't it?

Mwalimu Tombo: Yes, the neem is extremely hardy and drought resistant. Its seeds can also be processed into a safe natural pesticide. The neem is now being planted experimentally in the American Midwest and other semi-arid regions.

Prosecutor: Let the record show that in the latter part of the 20th century, desertification claimed hundreds of millions of acres of land, degrading an estimated 75 percent of rangeland and 20 percent of all arable land. Carrying capacity dropped by about 50 percent, leading to wildlife extinction and loss of biodiversity. The principal cause of spreading deserts, according to the International Panel on Climate Change, was modern agriculture, especially cattle raising, industrial pollution, and artificial weather modification. In Ethiopia, for example, land turned to producing linseed cake, cottonseed oil, and rapeseed meal for export to the Euro livestock market, produced chronic famine. The New World Environmental Agency adopted the commission's recommendations and has budgeted an average of $85 billion a year for reclamation projects. The New World Government's "Desert Sands Surcharge" for a fund to restore the world's deserts and compensate the victims of famine in the latter 20th century adds another $110 to the cost of every hamburger.

Noah: Mr. Tombo, doesn't the *Qu'ran* mention sand storms, and don't you remember sand storms in your country when you grew up?

Mawalimu Tombo: Certainly. I remember—

Prosecutor: I object, your honor. He is leading the witness.

Noah: *Sits down triumphantly.* No further questions.

Shiva excuses the witness. A young woman, in her early 30s, approaches the bench and is sworn in. She has on a colorful dress and shell necklace and carries a machete.

Noah: *Aside to the Judge.* Uh, oh, another Amazon. Don't they have anybody on a mommy tract in the 21st century?

Shiva: *In a low whisper.* Tell me about it. After Parvati took over managing the Burning Ghat, the household went to pot.

Noah: At least you don't have credit cards. You should see Kathy's monthly shopping bills!

Shiva: We don't have plastic, but we have something called the Green Exchange. It keeps track of debits and credits for environmentally safe goods and services. Parvati recently set up a chain of boutiques to merchandise tridents as a fashion accessory. She was so successful she's opening a Great Mall of China.

Noah: *Excitedly.* They still have malls! Kathy will love this century.

Prosecutor: *Impatiently.* The state calls Aii Xingu.

Aii Xingu: I am called Aii Xingu. I was born in the uplands of the western Amazon. In the days before the Great Heat, my family lived by a bend in the river, gathering wild plants, grasses, and fruits. Like the Yanomani and other native peoples, we had observed this peaceful way of life for countless generations since the First Parents, Ge and Ba. As a little girl, I was taught the healing power of plants and came to know the special gifts of each flower and tree. Then one day, men from the outside appeared. They had hard hats, carried some kind of strange black shells with which they could communicate long distances, and rode bright yellow creatures that devoured the land.

Fleeing for our lives, we moved deeper into the jungle. However, the destruction was terrible. We could hear the trees weeping and the birds and animals were frightened to death. A new species of spotted animals—something like a cross between a python and and antelope—were brought in to graze on the once lush topsoil. We felt sorry for these creatures—dubbed cattle by the men in hard hats—because they were prized solely for their flesh. None of the usual rites and rituals to placate their spirits were observed, and the whole balance of nature began to decline.

By the time the Earth Corps arrived to protect the remaining forest, many birds, animals, and plants had entirely disappeared. Fortunately, our family survived. But cattle ranching, mining, and logging continued. The Grand Carajas hydroelectric project and other developments uprooted thousands of people. When the Great Heat set in, we were forced to seek shelter in civilized areas and eventually went north as environmental refugees. By then I was married and the mother of three children. With my family and parents, we relocated to Ecotopia and now live in Gary Snyder National Forest, the sole surviving rain forest in North America. I am now a member of the bioregional assembly and chair of the wildlife committee. We now use a combination of radiotelemetry and traditional shamanistic methods to monitor owls and other endangered species.

Noah: *To the Judge.* Looks like she has found her niche.

Shiva: *Chants from the Gita.*
Attaining oneness with the infinite spirit,
radiant in herself, she does not grasp or grieve;

impartial toward all beings,
she obtains supreme devotion to me.

Prosecutor: Let the record show that Aii Xingu's experience is not unique. Two thirds of the world's rain forests were destroyed in the last century, primarily when land was cleared for pastures for beef cattle. Each hamburger, according to scientists, destroyed 165 pounds of living matter "including some of 20 to 30 different plant species, perhaps 100 insect species, and dozens of bird, mammal, and reptile species." In the early 1990s, economists calculated that each hamburger resulted in the loss of an average of 55 square feet of rain forest. That adds another $5544 to the cost of a hamburger.

Noah: I am truly shocked at the magnitude of the destruction in the Amazon and feel for Aii and her family. However, as a New York executive, I know something about real estate. Fifty-five square feet of office space on Madison Ave. or Wall St. wouldn't cost that much.

Prosecutor: Your honor, Mr. Wilson is talking about real estate. We are talking about the fate of the earth. The Earth Summit in 1992, you will recall, held that the deliberate destruction of the world's irreplaceable resources, including the rain forests, the oceans, and other microclimates, were the treasure of all humanity and that polluters were to be held responsible for the cost of their pollution. By the 1990s, according to Edward O. Wilson, the eminent entemologist at Harvard, 140 species of insects alone were becoming extinct every day.

According to ecologists, a climax rain forest takes an average of 700 years to develop, from seed to full canopy. The canopy, by the way, averages one hundred feet high. So we're talking of the equivalent of a twelve-story skyscraper—a higher average height than the New York skyline. Fifty-five times twelve comes to 660 square feet per hamburger. At at token value of 1 cent a square foot, compounded interest-free over that 700-year period, we get a total of $5544.

Furthermore, the Yellowstone Convention held that developers were liable for damages caused by the extinction of species. An average stretch of moist forest contained 1500 species of flowering plants, 750 trees, 400 birds, 150 butterflies, endless insects, and several dozen mammals. Altogether millions of different species once lived in the rain forests, representing two thirds of all life forms on the earth.

The priceless heritage of our planet—biodiversity—cannot be measured in dollars. However, as early as 1992, medical researchers reported that 1 percent of the plants in the tropics accounted for 25 percent of all medications, including 70 percent of cancer treatments. Economists reported that a typical acre of rain forest yielded $2500 in medicinal herbs and other potentially beneficial substances. This figure increased more than 100-fold in the next decade with the collapse of the American Medical Association and the ascendency of the American Holistic Medical Association, which was more receptive to dietary, nutritional, and herbal medicine. This adds another $2205 to the total for the International Biodiversity Fund.

Noah: *Takes out his calculator.* An acre is 43,560 square feet. According to my calculations, 55 divided by that times $2500 equals $3.15. I can live with that.

Prosecutor: *Taking out an abacus.* Yes, and multiply that by 700 years and you get $2205 like I said. Be grateful, it's not 7 million years—the time it takes evolution to naturally develop many of the species doomed to extinction. If we calculated on that basis, the price of a hamburger would jump by $22,050,000.

Noah: *Aside.* A mere slap on the wrist.

The economics reminds him of Jason and Maggie's reasoning, Noah becomes flustered, and starts to cough. Aii Xingu takes a powder from her medicine bundle and gives it to him.

Aii Xingu: This is ground from a root that once grew in my homeland. Just mix in cold water. It will help stop your coughing.

Noah: Thanks, it's so hot in here, I guess I'm getting a little out of breath.

Shiva: The court will take a brief fresh air break.

He pours Noah a cup of water, but he hesitates to accept it.

Shiva: *Laughs.* Don't worry. The water's free. Not like in your time.

Noah: *Notices the prosecutor inhaling something from a gallon bottle.* What's he sniffing? I don't suppose it's au de cologne.

Shiva: Bottled oxygen.

Noah: My God, they're selling air—the ultimate rip off. Is this what life has come to?

Shiva: They started bottling oxygen in Tokyo in the late 1980s.

Noah: Yeah, I saw that on the news.

Shiva: But that was on a small scale. Since The Warming, oxygen has become a big industry.

Noah: How much does a cannister cost? More than a hamburger and Coke, I'm sure. *Aside.* Jesus, there's a fortune to be made in bottling air. Why didn't anybody think of it before the Japanese?

Shiva: It's free! Everyone on the planet receives a ration of three cannisters a week at their local Global Village market, except of course those who live under an ozone hole. They receive more.

Shiva pounds his damaru to call the court back into session.

Noah: *Setting down is home remedy.* That's a funny looking gavel.

Shiva: It's actually a drum.

Noah: It's shaped like an hourglass.

Shiva: To remind everyone that time is running out.

Noah: There you go talking in riddles again.

A man with spry features enters and takes the stand.

Prosecutor: The state calls Glenn Hammock. Dr. Hammock is a climatologist at the Maurice Strong University in northern Canada and a Rachel Carson laureate for his work on the vole, the small rodent.

Noah: Your honor, really, what possible significance could the vole have on the price of hamburger? I suppose it eats meat scraps, gets hardening of the arteries, and affects the food chain in some way. But surely, there is enough hot air in this courtroom already.

Shiva: This is not a laughing matter, Mr. Wilson. *Raising his trident.* One more outburst like that and we will change the venue of this court room to Siberia or somewhere where it is really hot. Maya, put a tofu plaster on the defendant's head to cool him down. The witness will continue.

Maya proceeds to take a block of tofu, cut it with Aii Xingu's machete, mash and apply it to Noah's forehead, and cover it with a brightly colored bandana from the tropical rain forest.

Glenn Hammock: The red-backed vole is a bellweather species. To understand its significance, we need to look at the food chain. In its native habitat, it eats fungi and lichen on fallen pine and deciduous trees. It also has a passion for truffles and disperses spores of these mushrooms which inoculate in decaying trees. This in turn benefits squirrels and mice, and they in turn are eaten by spotted owls and other carnivores. Eventually the trees fall into streams and rivers, benefiting coho salmon, steelhead trout, and other marine life.

For many years, I have been following the migrations of this little creature, which was originally common to temperate latitudes of the Pacific Northwest and Midwest. Over the last generation, the vole has emigrated north in advance of temperature rises. In other words, even before increases in temperature are observed, the vole somehow knows when and where the warming weather will extend and retreats northward to find more pleasant surroundings. Thirty years ago, voles normally ranged as far north as Michigan. Then by the late 1980s and 1990s, they had begun to show up in large numbers in Canada. By 2010 Global Positioning Satellites showed they were almost to the Arctic Circle, as global temperatures continued to rise.

Despite these early warnings, society ignored the vole—with the most dire consequences.

Noah: *Aside.* Rats. I've got to destroy his credibility. Maybe there's something personal in his background. *To the court.* Dr. Hammock, could you tell the court how you became a naturalist? I think it will find your story most relevant to these proceedings.

Glenn Hammock: I started out as a logger in the Pacific Northwest. I was a real timber beast. I loved to go out and harvest trees, especially old-growth from the ancient forests. Then one day, everything changed. I went out to fell an enormous tree that I had marked earlier. In the top of the tree there was a bird's nest and a family of owls. I tried to scare them away, but they just sat there looking at me with their large soulful eyes. They weren't afraid or even angry. It was uncanny. They were almost human. The father owl came right up to me when I called. He was so peaceful I named him Gandhi. Well, to make a long story short, I lay down my chainsaw and bulldozer and never cut another tree. The experience led me to study wildlife and do something to help protect the environment.

Prosecutor: *Resuming the prosecution.* Mr. Hammock, what, in your view, is the primary cause of The Warming?

Glenn Hammock: Of course, there are many interrelated factors that led to a build-up of carbon dioxide and other greenhouse gases in the atmosphere. But every major environmental study in the last generation has cited the spread of cattle during the last century as the foremost cause. The world's cattle population reached nearly 2 billion.

Prosecutor: Could you be more specific about the mechanisms related to beef eating and the Greenhouse Effect?

Alan Hammock: Cattle ranching in Central and South America, as earlier testified, resulted in the destruction of nearly two-thirds of the tropical rain forests before it was halted. These forests, as everyone knows, serve as the lungs of the earth, absorbing carbon dioxide, the principal greenhouse gas that led to The Warming. As you have heard, a significant percentage of the carbon dioxide buildup in the previous century from industrial uses can be attributed to the production and packaging of animal food.

In addition, chemical fertilizers and pesticides used in livestock production produced nitrous oxide, another greenhouse gas, and cattle themselves contributed directly to this buildup by giving off methane. Methane, a greenhouse gas, is caused by flatulence or belching. The 115 million tons of methane produced by cattle each year were directly responsible for about 5 percent of the temperature increase. Gaseous ammonia, another product from animal manure, is a principal cause of acid rain, more damaging in some areas than cars or factories.

In many cities, meat was the single largest source of air pollution. In 1991 researchers at Caltech reported that cooking meat outdoors contributed to deterioration of air quality by releasing hydrocarbons, furans, steroids, and pesticide residues. In Los Angeles, infamous for its smog, barbecued beef was found to be the greatest source of fine organic particles in the atmosphere, substantially exceeding gasoline- and diesel-powered vehicle emissions, chemical processing, metallurgical processing, jet aircraft fumes, cigarette smoke, dust from road paving, and fireplaces.

Noah: Your honor, is he trying to tell us that a backyard barbecue is more dangerous to the environment than a Boeing 727 and a Mack truck? I find that a little hard to swallow.

Shiva: *Hands him some slices of deep-fried lotus root.* Here, take some of these. They'll help open your lungs, throat—and mind.

Noah: *Tasting them.* What are these, another kind of seaweed? Hmn, not exactly Dorito corn chips, but not too bad.

Shiva: Om, tat, sat!

Noah: Point of order, you lapsed into Sanskrit again.

Shiva: *Exasperated.* It means heaven helps those who help themselves.

Noah: *Taking another helping and passing them to the Prosecutor.* Don't mind if I do.

Prosecutor: Dr. Hammock, where does ozone depletion fit in this picture?

Glen Hammock: *Taking some lotus chips.* There are several important links between animal food production and thinning of the ozone layer—the earth's protective shield. CFC's, the cause of ozone depletion in the upper atmosphere, were used primarily as coolants in refrigeration and air-conditioning in the last part of this century until they were phased out by the Montreal Protocol. Historically, refrigeration developed primarily to preserve meat, poultry, eggs, cheese, milk, ice cream, and other animal foods which begin to spoil and putrefy immediately. In contrast, grains, beans, seeds, most root and round vegetables, and sea vegetables can be easily kept without refrigeration. Of course, some of the developing countries didn't sign the Montreal Protocol and proceeded with manufacturing CFCs. The New World Government's sanctions against Brazil and several other countries led to the short-lived "Refrigerator War." Following intervention by the Earth Corps, the Brazilian government reversed course and adopted a freon-free coolant system.

Similarly, air conditioning developed primarily for the convenience of people in modern society whose bodies become heated up by eating so much animal food.

Noah: Poppycock.

Prosecutor: Mr. Wilson, is it my imagination or are you the only person in this room who is sweltering?

Shiva: The prosecutor will refrain from such outbursts.

Glenn Hammock: People who eat large amounts of animal food can tolerate less temperature extremes than people who eat traditionally. This has been borne out in many studies among primitive people.

Noah: *Aside.* So that's why Krishna Deva, the cab driver from Bangalore and the Bronx who got me into this mess, didn't sweat.

Glenn Hammock: As a rule of thumb, about 50 percent of the world's energy that has gone into air conditioning in summer and central heating in winter is directly attributable to the modern diet. There is also a direct association between animal food and the deodorant industry, the largest user of CFCs in aerosol sprays until they were banned. People eating hamburgers, hot dogs, and steaks give off more body odor than those eating vegetable-quality food.

Noah: Fiddlesticks, I've seen some pretty raunchy vegetarians. Unwashed hippies didn't become a byword for nothing. I did the promos for Right Guard so I should know.

Prosecutor: *Intently.* You were involved in promoting products containing CFCs?

Noah: Strike that. It was purely on spec. My designs were rejected. I ended up sticking with detergents.

Prosecutor: *Going on the attack.* Detergents?

Noah: *Backpeddling.* Not your Jones bleach variety. You know, your biodegradable, cholorine-free, ring-around-the bowl cleaners. But really that was a small part of my schtick. My bread and butter—oops, soy margarine, so to speak—were static cling, hemorrhoids, slipping dentures, diarrhea and constipation, morning breath.

Prosecutor: Your honor, the state has medical researchers, fashion stylists, and other experts who are prepared to support the witness's testimony regarding body odor. *Conspicuously moving away from Noah's strong underarm scent.* However, I don't think that abstract comparisons will be necessary.

Shiva: *Sticking the trident under the Prosecutor's armpit.* I will allow no more personal attacks.

Prosecutor: *Backing away gingerly.* And what in your view, Dr. Hammock, is the key to slowing The Warming and saving the world?

Glenn Hammock: Of course, reorienting our modern agricultural and food processing system in a more natural direction is the key to slowing the Greenhouse Effect. And under the New World Government we have already gone a long way to that end. But I'm not sure whether, at this late date, we can fully reverse The Warming.

Prosecutor: How do you mean?

Glenn Hammock: According to all indicators, the trend toward our planet becoming a global hothouse is practically irreversible given the human impacts up until this point. Positive feedbacks from the interface between the atmosphere and oceans, cloud cover, the El Nino and La Nina weather cycles, the release of methane from the thawed tundra, stratospheric particulates produced by volcanic eruptions, the retreat of plankton to deeper waters, ozone depletion, the melting of the ice cap at the North Pole, rising tides, and other manifestations will result in continued global warming and a massive dieoff of life on earth in the next several hundred years, regardless of what lifestyle and environmental changes we humans are able to effect. The key to reversing this trend is stabizing the world's forests, and as we all know they have been dying off in temperate, as well as tropical regions, at a rapid clip. Like the war that was lost for want of a nail, the fate of the earth today may very well hinge on the survival of some lowly plant or animal in the web of life.

Prosecutor: And do you have any candidates for this role?

Glenn Hammock: Yes, the spotted owl. More than anything else, its disappearance has contributed to the decline of the old growth forests in the Pacific Northwest. In addition to carbon dioxide, the forests absorb, release, and regulate vast amounts of water to surrounding ecosystems. Their loss—accelerated by cattle grazing on national forest range—has contributed to the drying out of grasslands, wetlands, prairies, and farmlands, to intermittant flooding, and to the destruction of offshore kelp beds as silt from clearcuts washed into rivers and streams. A whole host of disastrous consequences on this continent and around the world has resulted. If tropical forests are the lungs of the earth, temperate forests are the stomach, regulating digestion and basic metabolism.

Noah: *Aside.* God, the owls perished. How could I have been so naive? *Contrite.* I never thought of acid rain as the earth's stomach pains, but it is a good analogy. Isn't there something that can be done?

Glenn Hammock: In order to fix the 5 billion tons of industrial carbon dioxide released every year, the New World Environmental Program set up an ambitious reforestation project in the early years of this century. About 7 million square kilometers have been planted around the world in Australia, the former Sahara Desert, the American Southwest, and other regions to offset human-made emissions. The New Forests, as they are called, have helped slow the Greenhouse Effect, but it is not clear yet that the trend has been reversed. At lower altitudes, oxygen-depletion and at higher altitudes ozone-depletion continue. Despite our best efforts, I'm afraid we have simply run out of thin air.

Prosecutor: Thank you, Dr. Hammock. Let the record show, in conclusion, that the effects of The Warming are staggering. Seventy percent of the world's population live within 100 miles of coastlines. Already an estimated 15 to 20 percent of the planet's 8 billion people have been displaced by rising coastlines, tidal waves, earthquakes, volcanic activity, and other manifestations of the Greenhouse Effect. This is not to mention the effects on other botanical life, from the plankton at the bottom of the sea which are killed by ultraviolet light, to the starving sea lions which have been driven ashore because of warmer waters associated with the El Nino phenomenon, to giraffes which suffered an epidemic of sunburn.

During the first inundation following the melting of glacial ice, millions of people lost their lives, livelihood, or homes as whole islands, archipeligios, peninsulas, and coastlines were flooded. However, over the years, humanity has unified to deal cooperatively with the emergency. Thanks to NASA's Earth Observation System (EOS), which launched a series of seventeen satellites from 1998 to 2017, we now have sophisticated methods to evacuate, resettle, and retrain people and help them readjust to changing climates and environments, such as the recent Phoenix Airlift, and today there is little loss of life and limb.

Still, the cost to human life, property, and humanity's cultural heritage has been incalculable. Of course, society has had to write off most of these losses as an Act of God in order to prevent the collapse of the world economy. Endless trillions of dollars have been spent—and endless trillions more will be needed in the generations ahead—to finish cleansing the earth. The New World Government's highest tribunal, the Earth Council, has assessed a Carbon Tax on animal food amounting to an average of $312.50 per ounce. This adds another $1,250 to the cost of Mr. Wilson's quarterpound hamburger. In addition, there are a Clean Air Premium, a Methane Allowance, and an Ozone-Depletion Tax which add another $350, $350, and $500 respectively.

High winds gust around the courtroom as the Prosecutor proceeds.

In the interests of time and safety, your honor, the state rests its case. We had planned to take testimony about the slice of genetically-altered tomato in Mr. Wilson's hamburger, the spicy mustard, catsup, and pickle relish, his soft drink containing tropical kola nuts and sugar, and the refined white flour in his bun. Suffice it to say that these ingredients, destructive to personal, social, and environmental health, add another $310 to the price of his meal. And as we have just heard, the tremendous changes that have taken place in this century are by no means over. The ultimate price of the folly of modern civilization—symbolized by the hamburger—may be the end of life on earth.

6

Shiva: *Chants from the Gita.*
Impartial to blame and praise,
silent, reconciled to his destiny,
solitary, firm in resolve,
the person of devotion is dear to me.

Mr. Wilson has informed the court that he will call no witnesses and confine his remarks to the closing argument, isn't it?

Noah: That's right, your honor. The charges against me are absurd. The sooner I am outta here and return to the 20th century and rejoin my family the better.

Shiva: But if you could have someone testify on your behalf, isn't there someone you'd call?

Noah: Sure, I'd call Gene Autry, Roy Rogers, or Hopalong Cassidy. They'd add a little balance to the one-sided views we've heard here.

Shiva: I think that can be arranged. *Confers with Maya.* Tex Waylor is performing in the Village. Will he do?

Noah: *Excitedly.* Tex is still alive and wailing? He was one of my childhood heroes. After appearing on *Bonanza*, he carved a lasting place for himself in the shrine of singing cowboys. *Hums the opening refrain to Bonanza.* ". . . Rawhide."

Shiva: *Instructs Maya to dial Tex on the telecom. A weather-beaten old man with a Stetson and reedy voice appears on the screen.* Evening, pardner. Judge Soy Bean here, somewhere east of the Pecos. We'd appreciate a few minutes of y'r valuable time. *Brandishes his trident in the air.* Little frontier justice to hand out, if you know what I mean.

Tex: Like your branding iron, Sheriff.

Shiva: One of my cowpokes, N.W., over here has a few questions he'd like you to answer.

Tex: Shoot.

Noah: Tex, I know you've been a cowboy all your life. Not just a singing cowboy and a movie star, but a real honest-to-goodness cowboy. I've followed you ever since you appeared in *Bonanza*.

Tex: *Starts crooning.*
I was born in a saddle,
had a live rattler for a rattle,
with my Pappy bred and raised cattle,

against injustice and foul play did battle . . .
Raising his voice and shouting to the top of his lungs. Rawhide.

Noah: *Whoops up in the air.* Whoopie, kai yai, kai ye! Tell us what it was like being a cowboy.

Tex: Son, it was a paradise. There were wide open spaces, clear as the eye could see. Every day we'd be up before the crack of dawn, rounding 'em up and moving 'em out. Rain or shine, hail or dust, we'd be out there under that big sky. Nothing compares to the thrill of having y'r pony turn a thousand longhorns as they thundered across the plain. Or the joy of delivering a baby calf at breeding time, or the sorrow of losing a fine steer crossing a riverbed. Or the satisfaction of knowing that families across the land are enjoying the fruit of their labor every Sunday after church by sitting down and enjoying a fine sizzling steak that you helped to bring to the table.

In the West, a feller became one with his horse and his cows and the land and the sky. *Aside.* Don't you repeat that to Betty Jean, my wife, you hear?

Cattle made this country great. No mistake about it, son. And I was proud to be part of it. Them Nashville agents and Hollywood executives, what did they know about an honest day's work? Or take those environmentalists who had never been caught in a flash flood or who won't go out into the woods without a beeper in their backpack? What do they know about nature?

Noah: *Beaming.* You said it all, Tex. Mighty obliged to you.

Prosecutor: *Rises to cross-examine.* Mr. Waylor, I've seen some of your films and would like to congratulate you on your fine performances.

Tex: Check.

Prosecutor: I seem to recall, however, that your country music and movie career came to an abrupt end. Am I correct?

Tex: *Buck Rogers, Star Trek, Battleship Galactica*—society turned to outer space for its heroes. The old West was left behind in a cloud of moon dust.

Prosecutor: That's not exactly what I'm getting at. The truth of the matter, Mr. Waylor, is that you got in trouble with the law.

Noah: *Shocked.* Tex Waylor, arrested! I can't believe it.

Tex: Yes, son, sad but true.

Prosecutor: Could you tell us about it, Mr. Waylor?

Tex: Sure, I shot up TCB's headquarters in Wichita.

Prosecutor: TCB?

Tex: Trans-Continental Beef. It's one of the nation's largest slaughterhouses. Me and the boys couldn't stand what they were doing to the cattle.

Prosecutor: And what exactly were they doing to the cattle?

Tex: From feedlot to supermarket, the whole process had become completely automated and dehumanized. The cattle were castrated, sprayed, chemicalized, stunned, and slaughtered without any regard to their welfare. It was a crying shame to see those big beef given shots of drugs and hormones in their ears, confined to cramped, contaminated pens and feedlots where they couldn't move around, and transported in giant truck trailers so tightly packed they often died on the way. In the old days, they had a real life. They had families and freedom of movement. Nearly every steer had a name, and by the end of a trail run you got to know each other, up close and personal. It was Bovacide, pure and simple.

Prosecutor: What about overgrazing? I thought that was just as prevalent as feedlot cattle.

Tex: Sure, there were both extremes. Under the BLM—Bureau of Land Management—the national forests and rangeland were turned over to agribusiness companies and their corporate stocks. Those computerized herds literally tore up the land. Topsoil, water, wildlife, you name it, it was near destroyed by overgrazing. The cottonwoods which I loved to sing about disappeared. Bunchgrass, sage grouse, Montezuma quail, and many others went on the endangered species list because of cattle run amok. Elk, pronghorn, and bighorn sheep almost went the way of the buffalo. Wild horses and burros and coyotes were shot to smitherines to make the prairies safe for these "hoofed locusts." It was enough to make a grown man cry what had happened to the land.

Everything came to a head one day when some rustlers snitched Chuckwagon, T-Bone, Wagon Wheel, Hoofbeat, Milkpail, and Bluebonnet. The first three were my prize steers. The last three were heifers, but darned if those hijackers with their CBs and laptops didn't take them too.

Noah: What happened?

Tex: We trailed 'em to TCB's main complex there in Witcita. We discovered that Chuckwagon had been pumped up with so many steroids he didn't recognize us. T-Bone had fallen in the truck, broke his pelvis, and already been put through the meatgrinder. Wagon Wheel had been force fed plastic pellets instead of hay. Hoofbeat and Milkpail had been rendered unconscious from the stungun. Only Bluebonnet survived, and she was about to be turned into Jello.

I vowed then and there I'd never touch another piece of beef, well, at least until justice and fair play were restored across this beautiful land. After a brief powwow about what to do, me and Sagebrush—that's my horse—and Peacepipe— that's my Native American business partner—and the boys, we rode in with guns blazing. We overturned the antibiotic and steroid tanks and set fire to the mountains of plastic feed pellets. We let Chuckwagon, Bluebonnet, and ten thousand head of cattle out of their pens.

Prosecutor: In the ensuing stampede, all hell broke loose. As I recall, millions of dollars of damage was done and seven directors of the company were trampled to death when a thundering herd invaded the boardroom.

Tex: What goes around, comes around, as they say around the campfire. They put me and the boys in jail and hauled our ass—pardon the French— into court. We got Gene, Roy and Dale, Matt, Lorne, and many others to testify on our behalf. Everyone agreed that the cattle industry had become bloated, corrupt, and a disgrace. Gabby, the Duke, Michael, Miss Kitty, and a lot of others who had gone on to the Big Round-up in the Sky would have been right proud. The jury found us not guilty and afterwords asked for our autographs.

Noah: Rawhide! That must have been some kangaroo courtroom, Tex. *Glaring at the Prosecutor.* I bet the prosecutor was a real tinhorn.

Shiva: *Waves his trident.* Cut the up close and personal, Noah.

Noah: Tex, I'm glad to hear you were cut loose.

Tex: Thanks, pardner.

Noah: You know, Tex, I had a small part in promoting the frontier myth. I worked on the Merrill Lynch campaign. You remember the bull who ran through the streets of New York? "We're bullish on America."

Tex: That was your handiwork, son?

Noah: *Proudly.* Yeh, they wanted to use a tiger, but I held out for the bull.

Tex: Well, I'll be darned.

Noah: Say, what are you doing these days?

Tex: Well, I've still got my boots on. Betty Jean and I run a wildlife sanctuary in the Panhandle. To raise money for our spread, we organized what we called the Last Barbecue in Texas. Folks from miles around came in their shiny new Cadillacs, BMWs, and Infinitis to enjoy a big hoedown. Of course, we had given up beef production, but old Chuckwagon had just died a natural death, and we figured he'd approve of donating his carcass to a worthy cause. At $10,000 a rib or steak, we made a pretty penny, and some of those old boys—and gals—so stuffed themselves that they bartered their fancy cars for another serving.
Our sanctuary now boasts some elk and antelope, and bighorns and pronghorn, mountain lions, brown bears, bald ea-

gles, and a lot of other species that are coming off the endangered list. Kids come from all over the world to see them. Of course, we have some longhorns, a few Spanish bulls for old time's sake, and the great-grandchildren of Chuckwagon and Bluebonnet. But the only barbecues we have now are with seitan, tempeh, and tofu. *Points to his heart.* Got to take care of the old ticker here, you know. So if your trail ever takes you out our way, come by for the biggest wheatmeat steak in Texas and a piece of Betty Jean's deep-dish blueberry pie with rice dream on top. *Sings.* Rawhide. . . .

The telecom goes off.

Noah: *Aside.* Jeeze, he was great up to the cross-examination. *Shakes his head sadly.* Old Tex must have eaten too much of Betty Jean's lean cuisine, gotten Alzheimer's, and grown soft in the head.

Prosecutor: Let the record show that the greed and cruelty of the modern meatpacking industry knew no limits. The effects on the land were devastating. One third of all the topsoil in the United States was lost from overgrazing. It declined from an average of three feet to six inches in some places, causing losses of $44 billion a year. Under natural conditions, it takes 200 to 1000 years to form an inch of topsoil. Soil that had been accumulating since before the time of Moses was lost in a generation of modern feedlot and range-fed cattle. Crop productivity in the West declined by 29 percent in recent years as the ecosystem was burdened by overgrazing, and countless species of plants and animals disappeared or declined.

The Soil Depletion Allowance adds another $350 to the cost of hamburger. As for Mr. Wilson's campaign on behalf of Merrill Lynch, it was precisely that kind of thoughtless advertising symbol—a bull running unchecked through the streets of Manhattan—that fueled unlimited growth and expansion and destruction of the natural environment.

Shiva: *Irritated.* The Prosecutor will stifle himself or the court will have him trussed up. *Prosecutor cows back and sits down.* Any more witnesses, Noah?

Noah: No, your honor. With defense witnesses like that, there's no need for a prosecution.

The Judge leans over and addresses twelve people in a side row. Each of them has on a T-shirt with the picture of a different animal or plant.

Shiva: Good, formal testimony is now over. The jury will listen attentively to the closing words.

Noah: *Shocked.* Point of order. Jury? Your honor, I thought you were deciding this case? Who are these clowns?

Shiva: Members of the jury, please introduce yourselves to Mr. Wilson.

Juror #1: My name is Alyce. I represent the oak trees of the forest.

Juror #2: Yo, Tim here. I'm a Panther, the former Florida variety that has been resettled in Maine.

Juror #3: I'm Nancy, a first-time juror. I am listening on behalf of present-day humanity.

Juror #4: They call me Nruka. I represent the Pacific Ocean.

Juror #5: Jimbo. Precious metals is my thing.

Juror #6 and #7: Wanda and Robin. *Holding up her baby.* We represent the kangaroos.

Juror #8: My name is Sundance. I am here on behalf of the fireflies and other insects.

Juror #9: Helen from the late lamented Troy, New York. I represent humanity's past.

Juror #10: Cary Frost from Berkshire. For this occasion, I am a prairie dog.

Juror #11: *A little boy speaks.* Todd Jeffries. I serve the children of the world and generations yet unborn.

Juror #12: *Man with black hornrimmed glasses.* Randolph Hunter. I am the foreman of this tribunal. I represent the Northern spotted owl.

Noah: *Aside.* Just my luck, my fate is at the mercy of an owl. *To the bench.* Your honor, this really is a kangaroo court. Why are all these people in Halloween costumes? I thought they were a grade school or reform school class doing their civic duty and watching the trial.

Shiva: This is the modern judicial system, Noah. Juries today are more representative of the earth than they were before The Warming. By lot jurors select species or planetary environments to represent. Three people represent the plant kingdom, three represent the animals, three represent minerals, water, the atmosphere, or other natural features, and three represent humanity, past, present, and future. Each person is sworn to represent the individual species he or she picks and the earth as a whole. It makes for a just, most equitable procedure.

Noah: There is a certain logic to it, I must admit. A world in which politicans and lawyers are extinct and threatened and endangered species govern! *Aside.* This will make a terrific movie if only I can get back to my time. Robert Redford, Harrison Ford, Michael Douglas—they would all die for the script.

Prosecutor: *Begins his summation.* Ladies, gentlemen, children, animals, plants, and others of the jury, the facts in this case are not in dispute. Mr. Wilson ordered the hamburger in question of his own free will and proceeded to eat it. No one held an aerosol spray to his head. Then conveniently, when the bill came due, he refused to pay it.

The State has established the true costs of his meal to personal and planetary health. They are all very reasonable, well established standards that have gone a long way to make the earth cleaner and more livable. Had we wanted to punish Mr. Wilson or make him an example for others, we could have invoked the principle enunciated at the Frankfurt Environmental Crimes Tribunal that just as it is a crime to take something that belongs to another, it is a crime to take something that belongs to everyone, namely clean air, water, or soil. We could have applied the strict standards of Ecotopia in the People vs. Hanford which held that persons or companies involved in the spread of nuclear toxins could be held responsible for damages not only for the next 360,000 years, or the lifecycle of Plutonium-239, but for another 700,000 years, or the lifecycle of Uranium-235 into which plutonium then disintegrates. Had we applied that yardstick, Mr. Wilson would be out not $15,000, but $15 million. Then there are whole areas we didn't get into such as the relation of beef-eating and the fashion industry. People who eat hamburgers, French fries, and other oily, greasy food require more clothing, more laundry detergent, more dishwater, more toilet bowl cleansers, etc. None of these things—things that fairly may be said to have made Mr. Wilson a living—were touched upon.

The effects of the cattle culture on the planet cannot be measured solely by dollars. Africa was laid waste, Latin America and Central America bulldozed, Europe and Asia decimated, the Australian outback and the American West eroded—all in the name of beef. As in the time of Moses, modern civilization has wisely rejected this golden idol from the past and gone on to create a society based on clean air, pure water, fertile soil, and healthy food. Despite all of the harm meat, dairy food, sugar, chemicalized food, and Frankenfood have caused, our society today still does not prohibit their consumption, as obnoxious as it may be. This is because freedom of choice in diet and health care is recognized in the Bill of Rights of the New World Constitution. So Mr. Wilson and the handful of other people like him are completely free to indulge their extreme tastes. However, they must pay for the consequences.

In Mr. Wilson's prime, the world was governed by the profit motive and CBA—cost benefit analysis. Today the economy of the New World Government is based on respect for nature and the harmony of all things. The guiding indicator is the HLA—health and lifecycle analysis which takes into account the health and environmental impact of products and services from raw materials and extraction through development and manufacturing, packaging and distribution, and advertising and promotion, to use and effects on personal and planetary health, soil fertility, natural beauty, climate, weather, wildlife, and the biosphere as a whole and finally on ultimate disposal and recycling. *Submits chart showing a breakdown of total costs of a hamburger to the Judge.* In today's changed world, the price of hamburger and genetically engineered tomato is high, but fair.

I respectfully ask you to find for the State.

Noah: *Rises to make his closing argument.* Men, women, children, and kangaroos, forgive me for not being familiar with proper courtroom etiquette here. Believe it or not, I have been transported here against my will.

The telecom flashes back to Scene One in which Noah is shown telling his wife, "Believe me in thirty years the earth will be completely changed for the better. Our children will be living in a paradise. What I wouldn't give to see it!"

In any event, one minute I was on my way to an airport to meet with some owls. *Becomes flustered.* I mean some trees, no I mean some businessmen with big jowls and talking to them about clearing out some deadwood in the office. The next minute I was transported to a Thin New World. I found myself in some greasy chopstick and bought a hamburger, not realizing I had passed into the Twilight Zone. In a matter of minutes, I commuted from a world governed by the Greenback Crisis to a world beset by the Greenhouse Crisis.

I may be guilty of time travel without a licence, breathing under the influence of a genetically altered tomato, or simple ignorance, but I did not commit larceny or knowingly commit any crimes against society or the environment.

Please judge me by the standards of my own era, not yours. Hamburger is an icon of my time, but then so were the movies, automobiles, television, baseball, and countless other conveniences and pastimes. By the same convoluted reasoning you have heard here, they could be held responsible for contributing to the Greenhouse Effect. This emphasis on one factor among many is bad science, bad business, and bad environmentalism. Nutritional correctness in one generation leads to totalitarianism in the next. The basis on which I am being based—affirmative alimentation—is contrary to the principles of justice and fair play on which this country is based.

I don't claim to be a saint when it comes to my lifestyle or environmental record. But I'm not exactly a sinner either. In the 1980s I donated my services to the campaign against Nuclear Winter. We designed 30 second spots for the major networks showing how nuclear war could drastically lower temperatures and kill all life on earth. Then the big danger was

Global Cooling, now it's Global Warming. Excuse me, if I'm still living in the Ice Age.

Politically, I don't know the motives behind this trial. Perhaps this is a test case of some kind. I wonder if I am the first person who has not plead amnesia or Greenhouse Syndrome when they've been caught eating meat—a practice I suspect is far more widespread than admitted.

Or perhaps, as an able and articulate prosecutor, Perry Mason here is running for the Earth Council or lobbying for a judgeship—very much like the lawyers and politicians in my era. Or perhaps his greener-than-thou attitude comes from some toxic relationship in his past like Dr. Salisbury. Perhaps he was a former Vietnam Veteran who went over the top on Hamburger Hill? *Prosecutor jumps to his feet to protest.* But that is speculative and out of order.

Or could it be that the Judge here has a conflict of interest? Could it be that global warming has caused his Himalayan abode to begin melting and the Varanasi ghats to overflow and lower real estate values? Nandi, his beast of burden in the parking lot below, is this very instant manufacturing methane and contributing to ozone depletion. *Holds his nose.* Krishna, his alter ego, is notoriously sentimental about cows. How impartial really is this court? You must weigh these things, as well as the evidence presented by the State.

In conclusion, let me appeal directly to the nine members of the jury who represent the animal, vegetable, and mineral kingdoms. As the evolutionary parents of mankind, don't look too harshly on the mere human being before you. In the scale of biological evolution, human genes and cells are very young compared to your own. I must agree that my era—my generation, my society, and myself personally—messed up the planet. I am ashamed to confess that I had a hand in what has come to pass. However, punishing me will not bring back any vanished species. Justice must be tempered with mercy like the acid—aciduous—rain. *Sits down.*

Shiva: The Jury has listened attentively to both sides and will now go forth into the community to talk with everyone about the case. Then after quiet reflection and meditation on your own, you will meet together and come to a decision.
Chants from the Gita.
Controlling their senses,

with equanimity toward everything,
they reach me, delighting
in the welfare of all beings.
Stamps his trident.
Court will resume tomorrow to hear your verdict.

Noah: *Approaches the bench.* This is quite some legal system, the opposite of the old one.

Shiva: It represents a change, but is not really so different from traditional society. The Iroquois who lived in this region had a Long House. At their councils, all major decisions had to consider how the consequences would impact the next seven generations.

Noah: Seven generations? In my time, business couldn't focus beyond the next quarter. Advertising and entertainment the overnight ratings.

Shiva: *Turning over his drum and chanting.*
I am indestructible time,
the lord of creation who faces everywhere simultaneously.

Noah: So what are my chances?

Shiva: *Rubbing his chin.* Of course, you can never tell with a jury. Kangaroos are notoriously sentimental, prairie dogs are surprisingly stern, and the ocean—recall Poseiden in the *Odyssey*—rather relentless when its vital interests are at stake. I'm afraid it's going to be a hard sell, Noah. Whatever happens, I caution you to prepare your will.

Noah: *Sinks down, thinking he faces a capital offense.* God, I've been postponing it for years. I can't believe they'll fry me. From the view of you are what you eat, kind of poetic justice.

Noah heads for the exit with Maya. Parvati, Shiva's voluptuous, eternally young wife, is preparing some food in the shade of a mango tree. She has flowers in her hair and is scantily clad.

Noah: *Mistaking her for a courtroom bimbo.* Hey, babe, what's cooking? Smells divine.

Parvati: *Handing him some rice and beans.* Try some. They'll help center you.

Noah: Say, are you a Taurus?

Parvati: Yeh, how'd you know?

Noah: The way that big bull over there is eying you and pawing the ground. I'm a Gemini myself. *Taking a bite.* Say, these are terrific!

Parvati: *Ladles out some soup.* Here, have some miso.

7

The next morning court resumes. The jurors file in to music performed by some of the witnesses such as Aii Xingu on the drums and Big Tofu on the saxaphone and form a circle around Noah. The Judge leads everyone in relaxation exercises and chanting Aum—the sacred syllable—together four times.

Shiva: Mr. Foreman, has the jury reached a decision?

Foreman: Yes, your honor. But before I announce the verdict, I would like to pass along an important vision bearing on this case.

Shiva: Without objection, so ordered.

Foreman: In accord with your instructions, I went into the neighborhood and talked with people, communed with trees, and polled other forms of life about the case. The general consensus was that the defendent was guilty, but that he was either suffering from GS—and what family hasn't had a member who completely lost their memory?—or was born with a low EQ—Environmental Quotient. A minority held that he was deliberately challenging the statutes of Adirondack. In fact, there was some suspicion that he was an agent provacateur of Sirloin.

Noah: Sirloin?

Shiva: It's a renagade province in Rio, the country formed from parts of Argentina, Bolivia, and Uruguay. Cattle ranching, biotechnology, chemotherapy, microwave cooking, and other trappings of lost modern civilization still exist there. The basic unit is the Pharm.

Noah: *Visibly brightening.* So the Thin New World is not so unified as it appears?

Foreman: After these town meetings, I ate very simply—just brown rice, miso soup, and a few greens as we are charged to do—meditated, and went to sleep early. In the night, a great Northern spotted owl appeared before me in a dream. It had an ancient, leathery face, piercing, tear-stained eyes, a chipped beak, and a strong, clear voice. The owl said to me very distinctively, "I am the last of the Northern spotted owls. This is my story. Many years ago, our species lived throughout the forest of the Pacific Northwest. Male owls, female owls, baby owls, grandmother and grandfather owls—all lived happily, nesting in centuries-old Douglas firs that had nurtured our forebears for countless generations. We lived in harmony with all other life in the ancient forests including mites, centipedes, salamanders, snails, shrews, butterflies, and folding-door spiders.

"Our timeless way of life rapidly came to an end, however, as human loggers came in and uprooted our homes. One by one, spotted owls died or were displaced. My eldest son, Big Beak, was killed when he became entangled in a plastic ring-top from beer cans left by the foresters. My youngest son, Spotty, passed away from pesticides in worms and insects that he had eaten. My eldest daughter, Moonlight, gave birth to offspring with strange birth defects. My dear wife, Pinecone, died from PCBs in contaminated trout.

"Still, we did not harbor hostile feelings toward humans. For generations, we had learned to live with native peoples who came in to cut down a tree for a house to keep themselves warm or to make a big dugout canoe to fish in. We learned to share our habitat with hunters who came to kill a deer, or even a bird of prey, for their meal when food was scarce. One of my ancestors, Spotsworth, sacrificed himself to a party of travelers on the Oregon Trail so they wouldn't starve. Another, Feather Shield, once saved the life of Chief Seattle by perching on the branch of a decayed tree inside which he had taken refuge. Soldiers pursuing him spied Feather Shield and figured no owl would remain calm and peaceful if someone were near. Most recently, Soaring Owl served as the model for human aircraft design. Engineers adapted the aerodynamics of his lightness in relation to wingspan to the construction of their own manned vehicles.

"We truly felt sorry for the modern loggers and their families who could survive only by destroying the earth. We could see clearly that by cutting down the forest they would destroy themselves all in the end, like the man who in his greed trapped and ate the last coyote.

"Still, we managed to survive and cling to life. Some kind hearted human beings who understood the interrelation of all things took up our cause. There were big debates and councils. Finally, however, the loggers and their allies brought in a clever medicine man form the East. He organized an 'Adopt-an-Owl' campaign to relocate the owls so that the trees could be harvested to cure cancer. The problem was this was an example, as Grandfather Owl's proverb has it, of 'Destroying the Forest to Save the Trees.' Spotted owls rapidly died off when transported to concentration camps and wildlife refuges. In desperation, my youngest daughter, Ena, and her mate set off across the Western Sea, where no owl had ever flown in hope of finding some new land.

"The corporations and families which had contributed to the 'Adopt an Owl' campaign received a certificate about their owls, complete with a photograph, cutsy name, and feathers. This enabled them to feel good about the relocations. But it did not address itself to the underlying issues.

"In the end all perished, except for me. I am the last of the line. I live alone in the last Douglas Fir in the last old-growth forest. The yew trees have also perished. The cancer cure—to the jingle "I Love Yew"—was short-lived because it didn't address itself to the root cause of the disease. Inevitably, the malignancy came back in more virulent form. But worst of all, the natural yew trees disappeared. It took the bark of six trees to treat one patient. The drug and medical companies reseeded the forests with millions of "superyews"—genetically screened seedlings, sprayed, thinned, and fertilized, which died out after several years from chemically-resistant beetle infestation. The result was only greater loss of life and misery.

"On behalf of the forest and the trees, the three-quarters of the world's bird species which are declining in population or are already threatened, and the other life, I humbly ask that you do everything possible to protect the earth." Great Owl circled above and flew away. Then I awoke. That is my story.

Everyone in the courtroom is deeply moved by the Foreman's vision.

Shiva: The defendent will rise.
To Noah, chanting from the Gita.
Armed with discipline, the sage subdues
and purifies the outer self, controls his senses,
unifies with the inner self of all beings;
he is not defiled even when he acts.
    So what say you, the Jury?

Foreman: *Puts on his glasses and adjusts them so he looks like an owl.* We the jury find the defendant, Noah Wilson, guilty.

Noah: *Shocked, he points his fan at the jury.* Could you have the kangaroos polled?

Juror #6: You're looking at the wrong beastie, brother. Kangaroos were displaced and almost rendered extinct in Australia by cattle, sheep, and other livestock.

Juror #7. *Her daughter wearing a Kangaroo T-Shirt.* Shame on you. *She does a little kangaroo shuffle, pulls a cannister of oxygen from her pouch, and turns her back on Noah.*

Noah: God, even the kangaroos voted against me. What about the Panther?

Juror #2: Yo, Brer Panther here enjoys a little juicy tenderloin once in a while and wouldn't begrudge a soul mate a bite. However, in these here proceedings, it was pointed out that the orange groves spread through Florida in tandem with beef consumption. Now these orange plantations wiped out Brer Panther's ancestral hunting grounds. Can't let that go down, now can I? It's all yin and yang, can you dig it?

Noah: The fireflies?

Juror #8: The Warming has increased the intensity of light in the temperate zones. Day is longer, night is shorter. We fireflies have been bumped from prime time to the reruns.

Noah: The prairie dogs?

Juror #10: Ad man, you ever have a thundering herd of cattle trample your hometown?

Noah: The Madamoiselle of Waters?

Juror #4: You're all wet when it comes to looking for clemency from the Ms. of Waters. How would you like to wake up every morning to the sewage of 2 billion people suffering from chronic constipation and diarrhea?

Noah: God, I can't believe it. The whole world is against me. What about history past? Helen of Troy, New York?

Helen: Troy was famous as the home of Uncle Sam, the meatpacker who became a symbol of the United States. Unfortunately, three quarters of the people of Troy, as elsewhere in the country, died of heart disease and cancer. Once we saw meat and dairy food for the Trojan Cow it was, we rebuilt our city—and our nation—on a new foundation. Today Uncle Sam is an environmentalist. *Takes out stamps from her handbag and holds them up to Noah.* Uncle Sam now wears green suspenders and his friendly face and hand beckon young people, "I Want You to Preserve the Environment."

Noah: *Sighing and sinking down in his seat. Aside.* I never stood a prayer. You can't fight the old red, white, blue, and green.

Shiva: The court will recess until this afternoon when sentence will be passed. Noah, you have the right to present any mitigating circumstances at that time.

Noah hastily scribbles a note and gives it to the judge.

Shiva: I'm not sure whether it's possible. But I'll do my best.

The court convenes for sentencing later that day.

Shiva: The defendent has asked the court to hear appeals for leniency from his family before sentence is passed. Unfortunately, Mr. Wilson, we have not been able to trace all of your family members. Following the Fiber-Optic Crash of 2009, many government, business, school, and other records were lost. Some have been reconstructed, but others are missing.

Noah: *Aside.* I hope they lost my IRS file.

Shiva: I must caution you that the information I am disclosing may be unsettling. But you have a right to know it.

Noah: *Confidently.* I can handle it. I am, after all, an adult.

Shiva: *Reads from file.* When the first big *tsunami* struck the East Coast, your wife, Kathy Wilson, was in the kitchen preparing breakfast. According to despositions, the house was destroyed, but she and several children managed to survive the giant tidal wave in a small boat that had been kept in the garage.

Noah: My boat, *Planetary Family.*

Shiva: The children were subsequently rescued, but your wife was swept away. According to one report, she was despondent about her failing health and impending mastectomy. No trace of the boat was found.

Noah: *Breaks down and weeps.* O God, Kathy got breast cancer! Why didn't she change her diet? Why didn't she take some medicine from the yew tree?

Shiva: *Chants from the Gita.*
You mourn for those beyond grief,
and you speak words of insight and understanding;
but the sage does not grieve
for the living or the dead.

Noah: *Clearing his tears.* What about my children?

Shiva: *Leafs through another file.* According to this clipping, your older son, Jason, became a star tackle for the New York Giants, leading the team to three straight Superbowls.

Noah: *Gives the high five.* All right!

Shiva: However, he suffered from cardiomyopathy, the progressive degeneration of the heart muscle. According to doctors, it enlarged to the size of a pizza. He received a heart transplant and went on to devote the years remaining to doing promotional work for the NFL. He was last reported helping set up an expansion team in Rio.

Noah: Jason had a heart transplant? And is now in Sirloin? I told him to hold the pepperoni. Mark?

Shiva: Your younger son, Mark, went to Princeton, then to Harvard for his MBA, and became an investment banker.

Noah: *Proudly.* Like father, like son!

Shiva: Unfortunately, he developed a drug problem and was blackmailed into laundering money for a Latin America cocaine syndicate. He turned state's evidence and was given ten years' probation. He is presently in a detox program at a Club Arctic wellness center.

Noah: I knew there was a reason I didn't want to meet Carlos "Big Tofu" Martinque in a back pantry. My son turned him in. What about the girls?

Shiva: *Picks up another file.* Your older daughter, Maggie, was in an accident.

Noah: Oh God, don't tell me she graduated from a moped to a motorcycle. She was killed in a crash and her vital organs were donated to fifty-two people.

Shiva: Shortly after high school Maggie married a local car mechanic. However, after several years, the couple remained childless and decided to have a baby by a surrogate mother. Several months after the baby's birth, the biological mother claimed the baby. Your daughter and son-in-law won the case, but the estranged mother and her boyfriend decided to kidnap the infant. During a car chase, your daughter was injured but not seriously. However, the abduction of the baby was emotionally distressing, and she has been in therapy ever since.

Noah: Poor Maggie, she ate too much ice cream and couldn't conceive. Didn't anyone turn out normal?

Shiva: I am happy to report that your younger daughter, Emily, is doing extremely well. After graduating from Yale Law School, she went into the field of environmental law. First, for the U.S. Environmental Protection Agency, and later for the New World Biodiversity Authority, she distinguished herself as an able investigator and prosecutor. She worked to eliminate drift-net fishing in the Pacific, helped protect the black bear in Asia whose gallbladder was prized as an aphrodesiac, and saved several flowers and vines in the Amazon from extinction. She also headed up the prosecution of criminal syndicates responsible for the international blackmarket in ivory, tortoiseshell, and materials from other endangered species.

By coincidence, your daughter is in the L'il Apple testifying on a maritime case, and she has agreed to come here today.

Noah: Emily! Emily's here and all grown up?

Shiva: I must caution you, Mr. Wilson, that as far as your daughter knows, her father died a long time ago. She will not recognize you, so please do not add to her trauma by identifying yourself or bringing up unhappy memories. We have told her that a civil suit has been brought concerning a friend of her late father and that she may be asked a few questions. Is that understood?

Noah: Agreed.

An attractive middle-age woman in a green dress enters and takes the stand.

Shiva: *Chants from the Gita.*
   Wisdom flows from modesty,
   truthfulness, nonviolence, calm,
   detachment from sons and daughters,

wife and home,
equanimity and gratefulness
in times of success and failure.
Ms. Wilson, could you tell the court your family background.

Emily: Yes, my name is Emily Wilson. I was born in Queens and grew up in Stamford, Connecticut. My father, an advertising executive, passed away in a plane crash when I was a little girl. My mother was a housewife. After Papa died, she went back to work, making cheesecakes and pastries for local convenience stores and other outlets. She came down with cancer when I was a teenager and was lost in the early years of The Warming. I had two brothers and a sister, all of whom came to unhappy ends.

Noah: *Approaches the witness stand.* Could you tell us something about your father. What kind of a person was he?

Emily: He was a real night owl. He did his best thinking at night. Advertising jingles came to him best in the wee hours. Of course, I was pretty small when he died so I don't have very many memories.

Noah: There must be something you recall?

Emily: Yes, there is one thing I remember.

Noah: Really? Could you tell us what that was?

Emily: Papa was very conscientious about conserving energy. He would take us to the recycle center every week with the trash and see that the bottles, cans, and papers were separated. He put an energy saving device on the shower, which infuriated Mom and Maggie, but which saved BTUs for the whole neighborhood. Once he made us an old swing out of a rubber tire rather than take it to the landfill.

Noah: *Aside.* I was too cheap to buy the kids a new swing.

Emily: Another time he took us to Walden Pond. Papa was way ahead of his times.

Noah: I sure was!

Shiva looks at him sternly.

Noah: I sure was happy to hear you say that, as an old friend of your family. Is there anything else you wish to add?

Emily: In fact, looking back, I think I became an environmentalist because of him. Once Papa gave me a little stuffed owl. I remember him telling me "to always give a hoot," so that's what I did.

Noah: *Tears roll down his cheeks.* That's a lovely story, my dear. I'm sure your father would be very proud of you if he were here today.

Emily's eyes also well up with tears and, overcome with emotion, she looks like she is about to faint. Spontaneously, Noah takes the little fan out of his pocket and begins to fan her. She looks at it and gasps.

Noah: Do you recognize this?

Shiva assumes a fierce pose, but decides against intervening. Emily carefully examines the fan and looks into Noah's eyes as judge, jury, witnesses, and spectators all lean forward in hushed anticipation. Noah's fate clearly hinges on her response.

Emily: *Excitedly.* Yes, I recognize this! It's teak!

Noah: Teak?

Emily: Yes, teak, an endangered tree from Southeast Asia. *Looking at Noah sternly.* Is this fan yours?

Noah: My daughter gave it to me many years ago.

Emily: Don't you know that possession of teak is a felony? I'm afraid that if you don't have a permit, I will have to detain you for willfully endangering the environment.

As she turns on him, Noah collapses on the floor, the little fan open across his chest.

8

Noah is riding in the back of an ambulance on the way to his home in Connecticut. Next to him is a doctor by the name of Brahma Deva.

Brahma: I was wondering when you'd come around.

Noah: Shiva is that you? Krishna? Where am I?

Brahma: My name is Brahma Deva.

Noah: You could have fooled me. You have that familiar blue look about you.

Brahma: I'm a doctor at Bellevue Hospital. You were rushed in for emergency treatment.

Noah: What happened?

Brahma: They said you passed out on the Triborough Bridge. It must have been the sweltering heat, isn't it?

Noah: It was rather warm, as I recall.

Brahma: I'm a pediatrician, but everyone is away for the Fourth. Admissions asked me to take care of you. I gave you a little fruit kanten to cool off.

Noah: I swear you look like this Shiva dude, except he had four arms and legs.

Brahma: *Quizzically.* Funny, your blood didn't test positive for drugs?

Noah: It's a long story, Doc.

Brahma: Tell me about it.

Noah: Well, it was right after I passed out during my trial. When I came to, this big ox, Nandi, was licking me with his tongue. It was as rough as sandpaper. Shiva was all balled up in a yoga posture nearby. When I regained consciousness, I noticed he had all these arms and legs. I thought he'd eaten too much biogenetic tomato.

Brahma: Did he assume a pose something like this. *Assumes a Dancing Shiva posture with his arms and legs.*

Noah: Yeh, how'd you know?

Brahma: *Chants from the Gita.*
When they see that a day of Brahma
spans a thousand eons,
and a night encompasses a thousand eons,
human beings understand day and night.
    Between the maternity ward and the ER, I've seen practically everything.

Noah: Anyway, Shiva went through this dance routine—you know, a little ballet, a little calypso, a little hard rock—where he kept changing form and shape. Finally he transformed into a great Northern spotted owl, the same one which testified against me earlier.

Brahma: *Puts his hand on Noah's forehead and with the other takes his pulse.* And just what did this big bird say?

Noah: Great Owl said, "My species is now extinct. I would do anything to spare this tragedy from happening to other life on this planet, including this poor human being here. Despite his past crimes against the environment, polyester pants, and other faults, still he is a creature of the earth. He has the potential for change. I did some pretty dumb things in my time like taunt loggers and filch picnic food, bringing down wrath on all my fellow owls. Who is to say, perhaps his genes—like his namesake's—will one day alone be responsible for carrying forward future life on earth? On behalf of the owls and other creatures of the forest, I ask that the court set him free."

Brahma: *Tears trickled down his cheeks.* And did it?

Noah: Judge Shiva assumed his normal self again—if you can call it that—and pronounced sentence. He said, "The court finds you guilty of foolishness. Not eating beef is the single most important step a person can take to save the earth. By nature, you are strong and able, generous and kind. But you tend to be stubborn and intractable, especially when confronted with your shortcomings. Rather than admitting your past errors, you questioned the integrity of the witnesses, maligned the prosecuter and court, and evaded personal responsibility.

"On the other hand, you admitted in your peroration to the jury that the earth was a mess and that you had contributed to the sorry state of affairs. Ordinarily such an admission would bring good behavior in the form of a 5 to 20 lifetimes' sentence of gathering styrofoam fast food containers from old trash heaps, conducting a census of termite ants and other endangered species, replanting a tropical rain forest, or cleaning the coils of old refrigerator coolant units with a toothbrush."

Brahma: *Thoughtfully.* We could use that kind of creative sentencing here in New York.

Noah: I didn't ask him what a stiff sentence would be. But the IRC—the Infrared Channel—of the telecom suddenly came on with panoramic scenes of forlorn masses of people pushing shopping carts in endless landfills. Credits at the bottom of the screen identified them as people who always took plastic rather than paper. There were also lost souls drowning in lakes of motor oil and brake fluid like ducks in an oil spill. They were automobile executives who had sacrificed better fuel economy to higher prices. I saw others perpetually climbing mountains of foam pellets. They were manufacturers and merchants who shipped their goods without bothering to invest in natural packaging.

Brahma: Sounds like Dante's *Inferno.*

Noah: Yes, but it didn't last forever. Take the scientists, politicians, and entrepreneurs who developed nuclear energy. These poor souls were condemned to wander barren and isolated regions with geiger counters to measure radiation levels for 12,000 generations—the length of time it takes Plutonium-239 to decay and become harmless.

Brahma: I guess it couldn't get any worse than that.

Noah: Don't be too sure. In the lowest regions, there were legions slowly roasting in giant microwave ovens. I asked who these hungry ghosts were and was told that they were those on earth who never took time to properly cook their food. In the microwaves, they were subject to 2.3 million oscillations per second—the same vibration food cooks at until its molecules begin to disintegrate and change form. Their only distraction was cable TV with remote controls on which they could switch back and forth between 155 channels depicting real food.

Brahma: And the Ice Hell—the ultimate pits?

Noah: *Shudders in recollection.* O lamentation. I saw pale shades strapped down or inserted bodily in cold metallic chambers. Masked devils hovered over them with sharp instruments, pricking their pancreases, livers, and hearts. When that torture wore off, they were bombarded with harmful rays and waves and injected with all sorts of posions. Finally, female imps in white disguised as ministering angels came in and gave them ice cream, soda pop, and other cold foods designed to destroy their kidney function, if they had any left. It was the most horrible place I've ever seen. Life was frozen. There was almost no human contact.

Brahma: Hmm, sounds like the surgery ward. You probably flicked on a rerun of *General Hospital.*

Noah: *Shivers in horror.* Maybe so. In an antechamber of this lowest circle, I came across some troubled spirits who had been reincarnated as adding machines, calculators, and computers. They were unhappy with their new station in life and were waiting for human heart transplants. One of these pitiful creatures—a pharmaceutical executive who still had a hard, steerlike aura—explained to me that he had been reborn as a CPU because in his past life he always put a price on everything.

    A companion, a former Secretary of Agriculture, had been transformed into an ice truck and was trying to barge to the head of the line. But it was so frozen solid, he could get no traction. "Natural justice," he explained in a feeble voice nudging me with a bumper. "I bragged before a political convention that environmentalists should be strung up and that the Northern spotted owl is ultimately going to go the way of the ice truck." I wept to see how far they had fallen, leaving them awaiting brunch—shredded spreadsheats garnished with bottom lines.

Brahma: So what was your sentence?

Noah: I thought for sure Shiva would lash me to his trident and sentence me to be held over a giant backyard barbecue and burn for eons. But Parvati, his beautiful wife, appeared with a big bowl of homemade mango amasake and said it was my lucky day. She predicted that her husband would soon be in a merciful mood. How she knew this I don't know, but she seemed to have him wrapped around her little finger.

Sure enough, a little while later, Shiva's fierceness subsided and he said, "As the *Bhagavad Gita* teaches, whosoever gives a leaf, a flower, a grain of rice, or a drop of water with devotion is dear to me. Noah, when you spontaneously gave the fan to your daughter, that was an act of compassion. You acted from the heart according to your highest nature without attachment to the fruits of your action.

"The price of such a selfless act is immeasurable. While I have upheld the jury's verdict today, I am deeply troubled by the tendency within society to calculate everything in monetary terms. Today's legal standards are fairer and juster than in the past. But ultimately, no price can be put on personal health, social health, and the preservation of the natural environment. The worst effects of the cattle culture are spiritual—and these were not addressed at the trial. Eating beef leads to overall hardening of mind as well as body. Vision narrows and becomes more materialistic. Life cannot be measured by dollars, BTUs, kilowatts, and other material standards. By eating hamburger, we lose sight of the infinite universe and its wonderful order. Each person, each family, each species, and each habitat has been profoundly affected by the excesses of modern civilization, and no amount of money can set things right. However, from such tragic experiences a deeper understanding of heaven and earth may emerge. Beings may become more grateful for their natural surroundings and learn to live as one planetary family. By the same token, the worst polluters and destroyers may also change in the course of time into the greatest angels. They are true teachers of humanity, testing its judgment, sharpening its intuition, and developing its wisdom and compassion.

"Therefore, Noah, in view of your meritorious action, I have decided to heed Great Owl's recommendation of leniency. The court releases you on probation with the stipulation that you mend your ways. *Shakes his trident at him sternly.* Before returning home, I strongly recommend that you go to Berkshire—that is, former New England. Visit the One Peaceful World Shrine, which draws thousands of people from around the world and is devoted to the health and well being of all life. Confess to the infinite universe your imbalanced past way of life, including past way of eating, and vow to live in harmony in the future. Enroll in nearby Michio Kushi University and study universal principles of natural order, including natural farming and food production, macrobiotic cooking, and other practical courses.

"Like your namesake, the Biblical Noah, you have the glorious opportunity to help save all the world's creatures. The destruction then was by water. Today it is by fire—global warming as the result of modern civilization's misuse of technology, especially the unnatural agricultural and food processing system, electrical and microwave cooking, and biogenetically altered food. The ark which will carry humanity to the new world is not a boat or physical conveyance of some kind. Nor is it the blueprint of the genetic code, or even a seed bank preserving traditional varieties of plants and animals. The ark is the unifying principle. In the Far East this is known as yin and yang. In the India, this is known as *rajas* and *tamas*. In the Middle East, Jesus referred to it as movement and rest. In modern science it appears as anabolic and catabolic, centripetal and centrifugal force, plus and minus, and other polarities. The animals in the ark represent paired opposites. By taking as many different qualities into your consciousness as you can, you will master the universal law of change and be able to guide the planet to a bright new world."

As Shiva and Parvati, who had pirouetted onto the courtroom dance floor, continued dancing—you know, a little twisting, a little waltz, a little rumba—a special bulletin flashed on the telecom screen. The newscaster reported that a Greenpeace research vessel had located a family of spotted owls on a tiny atoll in the Pacific. The researchers were astonished because the owls were believed extinct. The owls were found to be nesting in a coconut tree and included a mother, father, and four owlets. "The island and owls appeared right out of thin air," according to the amazed sea captain. "They were living on wild grasses, fish, and seaweed." The newscaster reported that a Tlingit shaman from Ecotopia was being flown to the atoll to communicate with the owls. If they consented, they would be returned to the Pacific Northwest to help restore the forest now that logging had finally been halted.

Everyone in the courtroom cheered for the survival of Ena, Great Owl's younger daughter, and her family, and for humanity and for life on the planet. "In *Genesis*, the appearance of the dove, a bird of peace, signified an end to the Flood," Shiva observed. "In the same way, the appearance of the owl, the bird of wisdom, signifies that the earth as a whole has developed the consciousness to pass safely through the present crisis. In the days ahead, as the forest ecosystem rebalances with the spotted owl's return, I would not be surprised if the earth begins to cool off and gradually the natural environment return to normal."

Everyone in the courtroom spontaneously broke into a large circle dance, linking arms and hearts. Waves of blissful energy filled every corner of the courtroom. I even embraced Dr. Salisbury, Aii Xingu, Big Tofu, the elephant-headed Ganesh, and the Prosecutor. There was complete oneness. Everyone was lost in pure delight, the distinction between self and other, species and environment, melting away in radiant light. On this joyful note, Shiva who was entwined with Parvati in a rather unholy embrace adjourned the court and indicated I was free to leave.

Brahma: And did you go?

Noah: The last thing I remember is buckling up in a little saddle on the back of Nandi the Bull. Oceanic feelings of love still washed over me.

Brahma: *Aside.* Must have taken some dynamite new type of LSD.

Noah: You know, the funny thing is that I came to love the food. Over the course of the week, I ate more grains and vegetables than I had in my entire life. I even came to enjoy Parvati's seaweed chips.

Brahma: Would you like to hear a poem?

Noah: You write poetry?

Brahma: It's an exercise we do in a rebirthing class I'm taking at Fordham. It just came to me. With apologies to Ralph Waldo Emerson's poem, "Brahma," I entitled it "Shiva," in honor of a cousin:

Shiva

If the nuclear scientist thinks he has conquered matter,
If the astrophysicist think he has fathomed time,
They know not well the subtle ways
I spiral, weave, flow, and mime.
The beginning and end of the universe to me are near.
Glacial ice and global warming they are the same.
The vanished species to me appear,
And one to me are CO_2 and oxygen.
They bioengineer ill who leave me out,
When me they splice, I am the genes.
The Nobel laureates pine for my genome,
But thou meek lover of the good,
Renounce biotech and find me in every heart and home.

Noah: It has a nice jingle to it. With the right visuals, it would make a good sound byte. *Aside.* What's a genome?

The ambulance pulls up to the Wilson residence.

Brahma: Well, here we are.

Noah: *Jumping out.* Thanks, Doc. I owe you one.

Spotlight focuses on Brahma waving goodbye with all four hands.

9

Inside the house, Noah comes upon his wife and kids getting ready for the Fourth of July party.

Noah: Sweetie, I'm home.

Kathy: How'd the trip go, Hon?

Noah: I missed my flight.

Kathy: You didn't get to Seattle?

Noah: It's a long story, dear.

Kathy: *Looks up nonplussed at his tropical bandana.* Well, change your headband and freshen up. Don't forget, honey, we have a party this afternoon. The Stedmans are bringing over some steaks.

Noah: Well, you can tell them to stuff it. And would you mind getting me the number of the Rainforest Alliance. I'm gonna offer them my services *pro bono*.

Kathy: *Incredulously with her hands on her hips.* Is this the same Noah Wilson who was ready to sacrifice the owls on the altar of modern civilization?

Noah: *Chants from the Gita.*
Better to do one's own duty imperfectly
than to do another's well.
Performing action according to his highest self,
a person avoids imbalance.
Thanks to Krishna, Shiva, and Brahma, my delusion
is dispersed.
By their grace, my memory has come back.
I return home, my doubts dispelled
ready to realize our endless dream
of one healthy, peaceful world.

The children come in one by one and welcome Noah home.

Noah: Hi, kiddos. Papa's home.

Jason: Hey, Pop, you got any dough?

Noah: *Takes the packet of freeze-dried bacteria batter from the pocket of his suit jacket.* Here you go, son. I brought you a dynamite pizza.

Jason: You're one cool dude, Dad.

Noah: *Aside.* And I intend to remain so. *To Jason.* Just add some water and pop it in the microwave. Oh and don't worry, son, if the anchovies wiggle a little.

Jason rushes off to prepare the mix which will devour the microwave. Mark, the younger son, enters with his stock portfolio.

Mark: Hey, Dad, what's up?

Noah: Soyaplus!

Mark: Never heard of it.

Noah: It's a little known holding company for the foods of the future.

Mark: You think I should risk it?

Noah: Sure, son, you need to diversify. You don't want to put all your high cholesterol in one basket. Dump some of those biotech stocks, for example, and invest in wildlife bonds.

Mark leaves punching numbers on his calculator. Maggie comes in. She is eating an ice cream cone.

Noah: Maggie, I've decided to let you get a Moped.

Maggie: Hooray.

Noah: The only catch it you have to pay for it yourself. *Takes the* *ice cream cone out of her hand.* Now what I propose is that you set aside your ice cream money and put it into a vehicle fund.

Maggie: *Mulling it over.* Yeah, I guess I can survive without chocolate for a few months. Boys and wheels, that's something else.

Noah: Good girl.

She leaves and Emily comes into the room, carrying her toy owl. She gives her father a big smile.

Noah: Hello, Sunshine.

Emily: Pop, what's ozone depletion?

Noah: What is this—*60 Minutes?*

Emily: No, Pop, 60 seconds. Please, it's for my science camp project.

Noah: It's when the air thins and you can't think straight. Your priorities get all turned around and you put things like money, career, and success ahead of life. You don't give a hoot any more for family or nature.

Emily: But what causes it?

Noah: It's a long story, Sunshine. I'll explain it at dinner. Is there a health food store nearby?

Emily: There's one in the village, Pop.

Noah: *Takes out some cash.* Here, sweetheart, take this and get as much tempeh as you can. And a couple packages of whole wheat buns. And some tofu mayonnaise if they have it. Papa's gonna make you the best burger you ever had.

She gives him a kiss on the cheek, flips him the stuffed owl, and races out the door.

The Beginning

Appendix 1

The Real Cost of a Hamburger

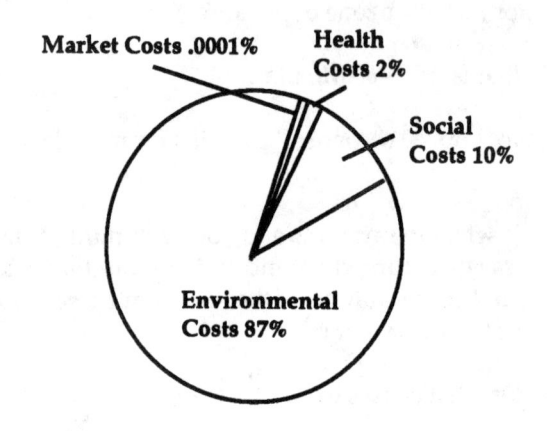

Market Costs .0001%
Health Costs 2%
Social Costs 10%
Environmental Costs 87%

Usual Costs

.55 Raw Materials
.47 Labor
.73 Overhead
.25 Profit
$2.00 Subtotal

Hidden Costs

Personal Health:

$13 Saturated Fat and Cholesterol Premium (Grease Guzzler's Tax)[1]

$273 Premature Death Insurance[2]
$286 Subtotal

Social Health:

$240 Superfund for Cultural Survival[3]
$194 Crime and Substance Abuse Surcharge[4]
$988 Peace Dividend[5]
$1422 Subtotal

Environmental Health:

$214 Clean Water Premium[6]
$350 Clean Air Premium[7]
$350 Clean Soil Premium[8]
$272 Desert Sands Surcharge[9]
$1483 Energy Surcharge[10]
$5090 Nuclear Deposit[11]
$5544 Rain Forest Tariff[12]
$1250 Carbon Tax[13]
 $350 Methane Allowance[14]
 $350 Ozone-Depletion Tax[15]
$2205 Biodiversity Fund[16]
 $513 Interest on the Environmental Debt[17]
$12,980 Subtotal

Other Items

$310 Soft Drink and Trimmings[18]

$15,000 Grand Total

---

1. Direct and indirect medical expenses including B&B, or Bypass and Biopsy costs.

2. Compensation for lost earnings over 30 years from premature death.

3. 80 percent of the nation's grains are fed to cattle instead of people, resulting in widespread poverty, hunger, and disease around the world; this special fund is designed to help the Third World recover from the spread of the modern cattle culture.

4. Assessment for alcohol-, drug-, and crime-related costs associated with the modern

diet.

5. Costs related to war and preparations for war associated with the modern way of eating.

6. An average of 300 gallons of water is used to make 1 hamburger; 80% of the nation's water pollution and clean up costs are related to animal food production.

7. Barbecued beef is the single largest cause of smog in Los Angeles and many other major cities.

8. Every hamburger results in the estimated loss of 35 pounds of topsoil; an inch of topsoil takes up to 1000 years to accumulate naturally.

9. Costs of desertification associated with overgrazing, including famine and death in Africa and other drought-stricken areas.

10. The equivalent of nearly 1 gallon of oil is used per day to produce animal food for every person in the United States. This figure reflects the real costs related to petroleum and oil clean-ups; mineral-depletion; and pro-rated 14% of the national energy budget devoted to animal food production, projected over seven generations.

11. Each hamburger produces a trace of nuclear waste, based on pro rated 14% of the global healthcare costs of nuclear energy and nuclear waste disposal, calculated over 360,000 years, the length of time Plutonium-239 remains harmful to the environment.

12. 55 square feet of biomass are lost for each hamburger produced from cattle pastured in the tropical rain forests; this tariff includes net costs of lost wealth generated over the natural lifespan of the forest, about 700 years.

13. Main greenhouse gas tax from CO_2 and nitrous oxide related to animal food production and destruction of the rain forests for pasture land; excess carbon dioxide remains in the atmosphere for 500 years.

14. 5% of the greenhouse effect is produced by methane from the belching and flatulance of cattle.

15. Cost to society for thinning of the ozone layer from CFCs from refrigerators, air conditioners, foam food wrapping, etc., over a lifecycle of 140-190 years, including an estimated 25 million additional cases of skin cancer and melanoma.

16. Hundreds of species have vanished in the rain forests, the American West, and other regions as a result of cattle production and many thousands are threatened.

17. Based on current and projected spending for clean-up costs over the next seven generations.

18. Real costs of a carbonated soft drink, relish, biogenetically altered tomato, refined white flour and additives in the roll.

Sources: Estimates by the author based on data from the Worldwatch Institute, American Association for the Advancement of Science, Science News, Vegetarian Times, and the writings of Michio Kushi, Jeremy Rifkin, Frances Moore Lappé, John Robbins, David Pimentel, Quincy Wright, and other researchers.

Appendix 2

Diet for a Warm Planet

Macrobiotic natural quality food, including whole cereal grains, vegetables, beans and bean products, sea vegetables, and fresh, locally grown fruit in season, is beneficial to both personal and planetary health. Traditionally grown, harvested, and processed, whole foods such as these benefit the environment and all forms of life.

The following recipes provide a healthful alternative to hamburgers, French fries, soft drinks, and other fatty, sugary, and highly processed foods. For complete menus and recipes, see *Amber Waves of Grain: American Macrobiotic Cooking* by Alex and Gale Jack (Japan Publications, 1992) from which these recipes are adapted.

Noah's Tempeh Burger

8 ounces tempeh, formed into patties
1/2 onion, sliced
shoyu
sesame oil

Sauté the sliced onion in a skillet for a few minutes. Add the tempeh, cover, and simmer over low heat for about ten minutes. Add a little shoyu to taste, simmer another couple minutes. Serve in a toasted sesame seed bun or sourdough roll. Serve with lettuce or sprouts, tofu mayonaisse, sauerkraut, or other trimmings. For a mock cheeseburger, add sliced, cooked mochi.

Big Macro

This vegetarian burger is very chewy and delicious. The wild rice gives it a wonderful fruity flavor.

2 cups brown rice and 1/2 cup wild rice, pressure cooked together
1/2 carrot, grated
1 scallion, finely sliced
2 tablespoons whole wheat pastry flour
sesame oil

Sauce
1 tablespoon miso
4 tablespoons tahini
1/4 cup spring water

Mix rice, wild rice, grated carrot, and sliced scallions together with pastry flour. Form into balls and then mold into patties about 1/2-inch thick. Pan-fry in a little sesame oil until each side is browned.

For sauce, mix miso and tahini. Gradually add water to form sauce. Heat gently over low flame for a few minutes. Serve on sourdough whole wheat bread or roll with lettuce and sprouts and other trimmings. Grated daikon can be served as a condiment.

Krishna's Fluffy Brown Rice

2 cups medium- or long-grain brown rice
4 cups spring water
2 pinches of sea salt

Wash the rice and place in a saucepan. Add the water by pouring it gently into the side of the pan. Add the sea salt and cover. Bring to a boil, lower the heat, and simmer for about 1 hour. (Try not to remove the cover and check on it too frequently as this will release steam and leave the rice too dry.)

Parvati's Deep-Fried Lotus Root and Seaweed Chips

4-5 medium-sized kombu strips
4-5 pieces of dried lotus root
light sesame oil

If very salty, dust off the kombu with a wet sponge. Break the kombu into 1-inch pieces. Heat at least 1 inch of oil to 375 degrees in a pot. When the oil is hot, but not smoking, add several of the kombu pieces or lotus slices to the hot oil. Deep-fry for 1 to 2 minutes or until crispy. Remove and drain of excess oil on a paper towel. Serve in a basket or bowl lined with a napkin to absorb oil.

Shiva's Amasake Shake

1 quart amasake
1/2 cup sliced mango, peaches, berries, or other fresh fruit
pinch of sea salt
roasted, slivered almonds

Combine ingredients, blend together by hand, and let cool.

Brahma's Strawberry Kanten

1 cup strawberries, freshly sliced
2/3 cup apple juice per person
1/3 cup spring water per person
1/4 cup amasake per person
2 tablespoons agar agar flakes
1 teaspoon kuzu

Slice strawberries, add fluids and amasake, put in agar flakes, and simmer until the agar has dissolved. Then dissolve kuzu in a few spoonfuls of cold spring water and stir in fruit mixture until it thickens. Pour into molds or desert bowls and let cool.

Glossary

Amasake: A sweet, creamy beverage made from fermented sweet rice.

Bhagavad Gita: "The Divine Song," the *Bhagavad Gita* is the most celebrated scripture in Hinduism. Part of the *Mahabharata*, a much longer epic poem, the *Gita* takes the form of a dialogue between Prince Arjuna, a powerful warrior who suddenly turns feint of heart, and his chariot driver, Krishna, who offers spiritual counsel and reveals himself to be the Supreme Lord of the Universe.

Brahma: Brahma is the Indian God of Creation. He is often depicted with four faces and four arms.

Greenhouse Effect: Global warming trend due to modern civilization's increasing production of carbon dioxide, methane, and other gases in the atmosphere.

Kali Yuga: "Dark Age," the fourth and current age in Indian mythology signifying loss of understanding, calamity, and disease.

Kanten: A jelled fruit dessert made from agar-agar seaweed.

Krishna: An incarnation of Vishnu, the God who maintains the Order of the Universe. In traditional Indian mythology, Krishna is depicted as blue in color, a strict vegetarian, and the spiritual advisor to Arjuna, the hero of the *Bhagavad Gita*.

Macrobiotics: "Long Life" or "Great Life." The way of health, happiness, and peace through biological and spiritual evolution and the universal means to harmonize and practice with the Order of the Universe in daily life, including the selection, preparation, and manner of cooking and eating, as well as the orientation of consciousness toward infinite spiritual realization.

Miso: A fermented paste with a sweet taste and salty flavor made from soybeans, sea salt, and usually rice or barley, used in macrobiotic cooking for soups, stews, spreads, baking, and as a seasoning.

Ozone: A lighter form of oxygen which produces a protective layer around the earth in the upper atmosphere. Also at lower altitudes, a constituent of smog and air pollution.

Parvati: The wife and companion of Lord Shiva.

Shiva: Shiva is the God of Dissolution and Destruction in Indian religion and philosophy. He is depicted with matted hair, carries a trident, and is given to solitary meditation. As the Lord of All Creatures and Lord of the Dance, he oversees the destruction of illusion, especially the individual ego's separation from the universal consciousness.

Tempeh: A high-protein, dynamic tasting soyfoood made from split soybeans, water, and a special bacteria.

Tofu: Soybean curd made from soybeans and nigari, high in protein and usually prepared in the form of cakes that may be sliced and cooked in soups, vegetable dishes, salads, sauces, dressings, and other styles.

Yama: Indian God of Death.

Resources

One Peaceful World

One Peaceful World is an international information network and friendship society founded by Michio and Aveline Kushi. Its members include individuals, familes, educational centers, organic farmers, teachers, parents and children, authors and artists, homemakers and business people, and others devoted to the realization of one healthy, peaceful world. Activities include educational and spiritual tours, assemblies and forums, international food aid and environmental awareness, One Peaceful World Press, and other activities to help humanity pass safely into a new world of planetary health and peace.

Annual membership is $30 for individuals, $50 for families, and $100 for supporting members. Benefits include the quarterly *One Peaceful World Newsletter* edited by Alex Jack, discounts of selected books, cassettes, and videos, and special mailings and communications.

To enroll or for further information, contact:

One Peaceful World
Box 10
Becket, MA 01223
(413) 623-2322
Fax (413) 623-8827

Kushi Institute

A macrobiotic educational center in western Massachusetts offering seminars by Michio Kushi and residential classes and programs in cooking, healthcare, and spiritual development. All seminars include macrobiotic/vegetarian meals. For dates, costs, and to register, or for further information, please contact:

Kushi Institute of the Berkshires
Box 7
Becket, MA 01223
(413) 623-5741
Fax (413) 623-8827

Beyond Beef

A coalition founded by Jeremy Rifkin and numerous environmental groups on Earth Day, 1992 devoted to reducing the number of cattle on the planet and lowering beef consumption by 50 percent by 2002 as the single most important step to ensure personal and planetary health. Members include the Greenhouse Crisis Foundation, Public Citizen, Rainforest Action Network, Greenpeace, Earth Island Action Group, Food First, Physicians Committee for Responsible Medicine, EarthSave, and many more.

Beyond Beef
1130 17th St. N.W., Suite #300
Washington, D.C. 20036

Recommended Reading

The Adamantine Sherlock Holmes: The Adventures in Tibet and India. Alex Jack. Kanthaka Press, 1974, paperback, $7.95.

Amber Waves of Grain: American Macrobiotic Cooking. Alex and Gale Jack. Japan Publications, 1992, paperback, $17.00.

Aveline Kushi's Complete Guide to Macrobiotic Cooking. Aveline Kushi and Alex Jack, Warner Books, 1985, paperback, $14.95.

Aveline: The Life and Dream of the Woman Behind Macrobiotics Today. Aveline Kushi and Alex Jack. Japan Publications, 1988, hardcover, $19.95.

Beyond Beef: The Rise and Fall of the Modern Cattle Culture by Jeremy Rifkin. Simon & Schuster, 1992, hardcover, $22.95.

The Book of Macrobiotics. Michio Kushi with Alex Jack. Japan Publications, 1986, paperback, $14.95.

The Cancer-Prevention Diet. Michio Kushi with Alex Jack. St. Martin's Press, 1983, paperback, $10.95; revised edition, forthcoming.

Diet for a Strong Heart. Michio Kushi with Alex Jack. St. Martin's Press, 1985, paperback, $10.95.

Dragon Brood: An Epic Play about Vietnam and America. Alex Jack. Kanthaka Press, 1977, paperback, $7.95.

Fire, Water, Wind: Revelations on the Fate of the Earth. Hanai Sudo. One Peaceful World Press, 1992, paperback, $8.95.

Food Governs Your Destiny. Michio and Aveline Kushi, with Alex Jack. Japan Publications, 1991, paperback, $12.95.

Forgotten Worlds. Michio Kushi with Edward Esko. One Peaceful World Press, 1992, paperback, $10.95.

Healing Planet Earth. Edward Esko. One Peaceful World Press, 1992, paperback, $5.95.

Inspector Ginkgo, The Macrobiotic Sherlock Holmes. Alex Jack. One Peaceful World Press, forthcoming.

Let Food Be Thy Medicine. Alex Jack. One Peaceful World Press, 1991, paperback, $10.95.

Macrobiotic Diet. Micho and Aveline Kushi, with Alex Jack. Japan Publications, 1985, paperback, $14.95; revised edition, forthcoming.

The Natural Dog and Cat Book: Healing Your Pet Through Macrobiotics, Homeopathy, Herbs, Massage, and Other Holistic Methods. Norman Ralston, D.V.M. with Alex and Gale Jack. Japan Publications, forthcoming.

The New Age Dictionary. Alex Jack. Japan Publications, 1990, paperback, $14.95.

Nine Star Ki. Michio Kushi, with Edward Esko and special contribution by Gale Jack. One Peaceful World Press, paperback, 1991, $12.95.

Notes from the Boundless Frontier. Edward Esko. One Peaceful World Press, 1992, paperback, $7.95.

One Peaceful World. Michio Kushi with Alex Jack. St. Martin's Press, 1986, hardcover, $17.95.

Physician, Heal Thyself: A Doctor's Dietary Recovery from Incurable Cancer. Dr. Hugh Faulkner. One Peaceful World Press, 1992, paperback, $7.95.

Promenade Home: Macrobiotics and Women's Health. Gale and Alex Jack. Japan Publications, 1988, hardcover, $18.95

Standard Macrobiotic Diet. Michio Kushi. One Peaceful World Press, 1991, paperback, $5.95.

Publications

One Peaceful World, Becket, Massachusetts
MacroNews, Philadelphia, Pennsylvania
Macrobiotics Today, Oroville, California

Books by Mail Order

These books are available by mail order from One Peaceful World Press, Box 10, Becket, MA 01223, U.S.A. Please add $1.50 postage for the first book and .75 for each additional book. Orders outside of the U.S., please pay with U.S. funds drawn on a U.S. bank and add 20% of total order for surface postage and 40% for airmail.

About the Author

Alex Jack is an author, journalist, and teacher. He has served as editor-in-chief of the *East West Journal*, director of the Kushi Institute of the Berkshires, and general coordinator of One Peaceful World. He is the author or co-author of many books, including *The Cancer-Prevention Diet* and *Diet for a Strong Heart* (with Michio Kushi), *Aveline Kushi's Complete Guide to Macrobiotic Cooking* (with Aveline Kushi), and *Amber Waves of Grain* (with Gale Jack). Alex has taught macrobiotics and planetary medicine in China, Russia, and other countries. He is presently teaching at the Kushi Institute and directing One Peaceful World Press. He lives in the Berkshires with his wife, Gale, a macrobiotic cooking teacher, and their two children, Masha and Jon.